HÉLÈNE DU COUDRAY

Another Country

ALSO BY HÉLÈNE HÉROYS

as H. du Coudray

The Brief Hour

Electra

Metternich
(biography)

as M. W. Waring

The Witnesses

HÉLÈNE DU COUDRAY

Another Country

Published in 2003 by
The Maia Press Limited
82 Forest Road
London E8 3BH
www.maiapress.com

First published in 1928 by
Philip Allan & Co. Ltd

ISBN 1 904559 04 2

A CIP catalogue record for this book is available
from the British Library

Printed and bound in Great Britain by Thanet Press

'Thou hast committed
Fornication – but that was in another country,
And besides, the wench is dead.'

Christopher Marlowe, *The Jew of Malta*

To G. M. S.

PART ONE

I

WHEN THE P&O LINER *Garrick* left Malta in February, 1922, on her way to London from the East, her second officer, Charles Ronald Wilson, remained on shore. Dysentery in a small Chinese port had forced sick leave on him, and it had been decided that he should spend it in Malta instead of coming back to the vagaries of an English spring. He loathed Malta, which irritated him by the violent colours of its scenery and the partly Eastern, partly English atmosphere of its towns; but he consented to the plans made for him by the solicitous captain of the *Garrick*, and his wife in England, because he had not sufficient interest in himself to decide anything independently of others. He lost that habit – if he ever had it at all – even before his marriage. For Charles had been as unfortunate in his wife as in other things.

The son of a struggling parson who made up for the disappointments of life by frequent insobriety, he had been sent to a school 'for the sons of clergymen', where principles of virtue and moderate religious fervour were firmly inculcated into future pillars of the Church. Shy, stupid, shortsighted, and ugly, Charles had patiently borne the irksome burden of discipline and continuous teaching till the Headmaster suggested the sea as the only remedy for a boy completely unfit for public school life.

'Why, Sir,' the reverend gentleman had exclaimed in the interview which decided Charles's future, 'the boy takes no interest in rugger, and in the fifth form his Latin is too bad to be even funny, or so his housemaster tells me. The Church does not want blockheads, Sir. Try him in the Merchant Service. They might brighten him up a bit.'

So Charles was put into the Merchant Service to be brightened up, and in the Merchant Service he remained. In the course of time he rose with patient endeavour to the rank of 'second officer' and sailed regularly between England and China. The war wrought no change in his life except that in 1914, when home on leave, he fulfilled the expectations of his family by marrying Lucy, the only daughter of the late only solicitor of Elmshurst-on-Trent, to whose memory his sorrowing widow had erected a handsome monument, before betaking herself and a considerable fortune to the highly respectable suburb of Golders Green.

Charles, shortly after the birth of his second child, was able to thank the Providence which sent him into the Merchant Service; for thus he escaped (more legitimately than many) from the tyranny of his wife and the interference of his mother-in-law. Not that Lucy was a bad woman, but she had 'push', and Charles got pushed along with everything else. All day her voice, by turns persuasive, angry, and scornful, but always high-pitched and loud, rang through the small flat at 3, Michael Mansions, Bayswater.

'Tommy, don't climb up on that chair, dear – and shut the door, Molly, when you come in. Mummy is busy now and little Molly must be good. Run down and give the organ-grinder a penny; but mind the stairs.' – A momentary pause, and then without the caressing whine which always accompanied her remarks to the children:

'Charles, for heaven's sake stop whistling through your teeth. I tried to mend those socks of yours, but it's no good. You've worn the heels right through. Oh, *do* stop fidgeting; haven't I enough work to do without stopping to look for your gloves? Mind that curtain, it's torn. Lord only knows why I married such a clumsy idiot! If you go on jingling that money I'll throw something at you.' Sometimes a hard object picked up at random from the furniture would follow; but on the whole rarely, for Lucy, though garrulous, really had a placid disposition and bore with the trial of a dull husband and the rapid loss of girlish prettiness with great patience.

On that particular morning when the *Garrick* sailed, Charles loitered about the quay, his thoughts on his wife and the small, over-furnished flat in Bayswater. He did not often indulge in reminiscence; but today, when there were still several hours separating him from his next meal, his mind naturally turned to this unpleasant subject. He was bored. The Maltese winter had already dwindled into spring, covering the hillsides with flowers; but the beauty of this fragile blossoming did not touch him. He disliked the country and he detested sight-seeing. When groups of tourists laden with guide books passed him, he scowled and stared glumly at the sea, cursing the recent illness which condemned him to the island for two and a half months. So absorbed was he in his ill-humour that he started when a voice hailed him. He turned to see a little man with a hat in one hand and a stick in the other hurrying towards him. Charles recognised him as the Russian he had met a year ago in Bombay. The business of selling lace made by the natives of Madagascar had carried him all over the world. Once an officer in the Russian Army, he had, since his exile after the Revolution in Russia, drifted into commerce and married a native woman. Lace no doubt served as a convenient label for his many doings, but he was honest, and even his enemies could accuse him of nothing worse than a certain sprightliness and acumen which always caused him to be the first on the spot when there was hope of making money. To his friends he was no more or less than Homoutov, the reliable, obliging, and never ill-humoured young man (he was one of those who even in middle age keep the epithet 'young'), who was often generous enough to forget old debts, and who would even crown his generosity with a present of lace or Italian wine.

He approached Charles with his usual exuberance, greeting him with a stream of tolerably good English. What on earth was he, Wilson, doing in this godforsaken hole? He looked ill. Had been ill? – Oh, dysentery. Yes, he had noticed it at once. Had he at least friends who would look after him and entertain him? – Didn't know a soul! A great pity – but now, since they had met so fortunately, he would introduce him. He knew English people, even; but especially one family – Russian, charming. There were so many Russians in Malta, but Charles would like these. Would he come now?

– No, perhaps now would be too near lunch time – but in the afternoon. He was going there himself, to say goodbye before he left for Madagascar, and Charles could come too. The walk would be pleasant. Thank God, it wasn't too hot yet. Had Charles been here in July? – It was worse than anything he knew, with the heat, the dust and the winds; but now, of course, it was lovely; there were flowers everywhere, wild flowers – he loved wild flowers. It was very sad that there were none like that in Madagascar. . . .

At last he had to stop for want of breath and Charles ceased fidgeting with his pince-nez. He did not wear them often, but he had a habit of putting them on and taking them off again with a nervous gesture when he was impatient or out of sorts. He liked Homoutov, but his natural shyness made him recoil from the thought of accompanying him on his farewell visits to Russian friends. At a loss for an excuse, he muttered something about being busy.

'Busy!' cried Homoutov with a guffaw which made a passing lady look round, and jerked Charles's pince-nez off his nose.

'Busy, my dear fellow' (he pronounced it 'fellah' in the belief that it was very English to do so). 'Do you mean that you have already found yourself a pretty little Maltese? Oh, you English! – You are so quiet; but you are very quick.'

'My dear Homoutov! '

Charles was indignant, not because he felt insulted, but because he always shrank from the man-to-man frankness which Homoutov, perhaps in memory of Army days, liked to adopt.

'You forget I am a married man with responsibilities. Do

15

you think I am stuck here for two months with half-pay and nothing to do, for my own amusement? You Russians . . .'

'You forget you know no others except myself.' Homoutov shrugged his shoulders, and then, fingering his clipped little moustache, added –

'Anyway, you might just as well come with me this afternoon. It will make you forget your "spleen". One always has it after an illness. It used to be terrible in the war. I remember in 1915 when our regiment was in the trenches near . . .' But Charles, who knew the length to which such stories ran, cut him short.

'I must go now. See you this afternoon. We'll meet round here.'And turning his back on him he walked away in the direction of the Strada Reale.

Homoutov had not dissipated his gloom. He felt dejected and – a thing which rarely happened to him – preoccupied with the future. There were the children to think about. Half tender, half resentful, a memory of his wife flashed through his mind. Often when she was busy fussing in the stuffy kitchen, or over the gimcracks in the drawing room, the striped blouse she always wore came undone, weighed down by its heavy buttons; and he remembered how one day, in a sudden moment of passion, he had covered her bared neck and thin, bony shoulders with kisses. But the smell of her hair was unpleasant, and besides, she was losing all her good looks.

'Poor Lucy!' he thought, as he meditatively kicked a pebble along the pavement. 'She is silly, but she has had a hard life with those kids – and me,' he added as an afterthought.

They started out to the Villa San Michele (that was the name of the house) later than they had intended, because Homoutov insisted upon going out of his way to buy some fruit in one of the markets.

'Just a small present,' he said. 'They have always been very kind to me. True friends, you know!' Of these he had a great many. There was not one of his acquaintance, however slight, who had not, at one time or another, been distinguished by the label of 'true friend'.

They set out at last, toiling up endless narrow streets full of dirty children who sat about in squabbling groups or chased each other up and down. The shadows that had lain in firm, angular shapes on the walls were beginning to grow longer, and only the flat roofs of the houses gleamed in the sunlight. Swallows swarmed in the sky. Here and there dogs barked at them, and a beggar, rousing himself from his slumber in a doorway, mechanically stretched out a hand at the sound of approaching footsteps, and then again dropped off into sleep.

At last the paved street gave place to a gravel road. Houses grew fewer. Most of them were surrounded by gardens. Charles noticed that the oleanders had already put out their flat, broad leaves. They turned up a steep path covered with loose stones and stopped before a low gate. Homoutov paused to regain his breath; then led the way, through the gate and up another path broken by irregular stone steps. On one side of them was a wall; on the other a piece of ground which once might have been laid out as a garden. But it had been neglected and was much overgrown by convolvulus and the wild poppy. The grass smelt very sweet and there was a furtive rustling in the crevices of the

17

stone wall where the lizards were bringing up their young. The house, at first concealed by the windings of the path, appeared suddenly: a low, one-storeyed building, which had once been white, but now had a peculiar yellowish colour which made it look as though it was always in the light of some special, never-setting sun. It was like every country house in Malta: flat-roofed and shuttered. It, too, like the garden, had an air of neglect. Charles, who had an ordered mind that was disturbed by untidiness, noticed that the loose Maltese stone was crumbling off the walls, because there were bits of it on the path, and that the paint on the door was scratched. Homoutov did not stop to ring the bell (it was obviously broken) or call somebody, but only said: 'We'll go straight in; they have no servants,' and plunged into the semi-darkness of the passage.

Charles followed with a shrinking heart. To the word 'Russian' his mind now added the connotation 'refugees', and the thought was not at all reassuring. He was born in that class which hates extreme poverty only less than great riches, and avoids contact with the one, while it abuses and reviles the other. Without ever having thought about it, he instinctively felt that these people expected something from the world, which was under no obligation to help them. Of course they would imagine that he, too, came as a future benefactor. They might want to borrow money – he had heard that they were very casual about money matters. It would be most awkward. Why on earth had Homoutov brought him, if not for that? He was one of them too, of course, but the word 'refugee' somehow did not apply to him. He was too busy, too independent; his ready-made clothes were so neat, and his stiff little moustache seemed grown expressly to inspire confidence.

Stumbling through a passage lined with boxes and trunks, they came to a door which Homoutov opened without knocking.

'Ah, Pavel Andreivitch!' said a woman's voice, and feeling awkward, like someone who has inadvertently strayed into an unknown house, Charles slid round the door.

'I have brought an English friend – Mr Wilson, Madame Leonidov.' To his great relief Homoutov spoke in English. Charles bowed, seized an outstretched hand, shook it, as he at once realised, with unnecessary vigour, and sank into a chair, conscious only of the fact that his hands felt clammy and his bootlace had come undone. He cursed himself for having come, for having behaved like a gawky fool and for being unable to see anything in a room protected from the sun by half-closed shutters. A ray of white light lay like a stripe across the floor and the wall opposite him. He fumbled in his pockets for his spectacles, and found he had left them at home. His chair was low and he could not dispose of his legs with any degree of comfort. Homoutov and the lady were speaking together in Russian. When at last Charles looked at her, he saw that she was sitting at a table which occupied one side of the room. Apparently she had been playing patience, because the cards were scattered over the dull green cloth of the table. Her black dress showed up her fair hair and the pallor of her face, to which the half-light lent a yellowish tinge. Involuntarily he compared her to a large, sleepy animal. Her movements, as she arranged the folds of her dress or pushed aside the cards strewn over

19

the table, were quiet, deliberate, almost stealthy, like a cat's. Fascinated, Charles watched her white, rather plump hand playing with a knave of hearts. It suddenly made him think of his wife. She had yellow hair mercilessly crimped at the sides. Her hands were rather coarse; she had chilblains in the winter. He almost jumped when he heard a voice – it was rather low – speaking to him.

'How kind that you have come to visit us. We live so far from Valletta that even our friends forget us'– this with a look at Homoutov. 'And we know not many English. I speak English not often; but my daughter has a governess – she speaks well.'

She paused, evidently expecting some remark from him. Uneasily he cleared his throat, not knowing whether to say that she spoke well, or that he was sure the daughter did.

'You will have some tea with us?' she continued. 'The others will come in soon. Pavel Andreivitch, shall we not open the shutters? It is too dark, and my headache is better now. Mr Wilson will like to have more light.' She raised one hand to her brow and, with a decided movement of the other, shuffled the cards together and set the pack aside, as though to show her determination not to occupy herself with them any longer.

Homoutov pushed back the shutters. The transparent golden light of the late afternoon crept over the boards of the floor and the green distempered walls. It made Madame Leonidov's hair gleam, and filled the room with iridescent dust. Charles suddenly realised that he was sitting near the window and instinctively looked out to see if there was a view. From early childhood he had been trained to acknowledge the aesthetic value of those points of vantage which reveal distance to the eye. When guests were shown over the Vicarage at Elmshurst-on-Trent, his mother never failed to say: 'And this is the spare room. It is rather small, but there is such a lovely view.'

He remembered it well: fields, hedges, a few houses with brown roofs, then more fields, more hedges, bound by a grey horizon behind an undulating hill which was called a down. The grey monotony of it was present in his mind now, as he gazed at the white towns sloping towards the sea. Below him, in the garden, the shadows of blossoming almond trees lay in pale, skeleton-like patterns on the grass. Away to the left, beyond the shining expanse of the Marsamuscetto Bay, was Sliema – a wilderness of roofs: to the right, the harbour twining in and out of the land, which jutted out in thin curved tongues. The slender boats darting to and fro between the island fort Manoel, and Valletta, looked in the distance like those insects which, on summer days, flit across the surface of stagnant water. The sea curved towards the horizon, reflecting (like a vast prism) the colours of the sky, which glowed red in the West, but paled into translucent green where the moon was to rise, over the ridge of coast beyond Ricasoli Point.

Madame Leonidov joined Charles at the window and stood motionless in an attitude of ecstasy.

'Is it not beautiful?' she murmured. 'This is my consolation in my exile, Mr Wilson.' (She pronounced it with an emphasis on the 'n'.) 'I am assured you English cannot love Nature as we do. Have you anything as beautiful in your own land?'

'Well, the English countryside . . .' but Madame was not listening. The front door banged and there were steps and voices outside. Anxious to get away before anyone else appeared (he remembered her remarks about 'the others' with dread), Charles glanced at Homoutov, who had settled down on a high-backed sofa with squat legs and took no notice of his meaning look. Just then the door opened to let in a girl, followed by a man with a short, pointed beard and a very high, receding forehead. There was a dejected, forlorn air about his thin, drooping figure. His trousers sagged at the knees. He walked with a curious ambling gait that made the stoop of his shoulders seem greater than it was. He ignored Charles and Madame Leonidov, but went straight up to Homoutov and, without shaking hands, began to talk rapidly in a nasal voice. The girl, whom Charles guessed to be about twelve years old, was plain, with straight flaxen hair like her mother's.

'Ah, and here is my Irochka!' exclaimed Madame Leonidov. 'Come here, *mon enfant*. This is Mr Wilson, who is English. Our dear Pavel Andreivitch is his friend. You like speaking English, don't you? Show us how much you have learnt with Maria Ivanovna.'

But Irochka only looked sullen, and, without vouchsafing a reply, escaped from her mother and rushed to the table, where she began to empty the sugar basin – apparently the last trace of a former meal – with astonishing rapidity. Madame Leonidov gave her an indulgent smile, and, resuming her seat, opened a conversation with Charles about the beauties of Malta. Every time she moved her head or made a gesture with her hands, Charles wondered at her fairness and the statuesque proportions of her large firmly-moulded body. He had never seen a woman with such pale gleaming hair, such pale liquid eyes, and a face so pale that her lips were like a thin brown line across it. He noticed that when she smiled (which she did frequently; even when there seemed no need to smile) her mouth alone moved, showing large even teeth of the same yellowish colour as her skin. Her eyes never lost their cold, expressionless gleam. Her voice seemed the only living thing about her. It was deep and full, and she used it with conscious pleasure. She spoke as though she were always listening to herself. Again Charles thought that she was like a large, sleepy animal – a cat with a beautiful human voice. He was so absorbed in thinking about her that he hardly noticed a woman who came in with a tray of cups and saucers and was greeted by a laconic 'Ah, Maria Ivanovna,' by Madame Leonidov.

Tea followed round the table. Only the man with the beard did not join them, but sat on the sofa drinking tea in a glass against which he clicked his nails. The talk was desultory. Madame Leonidov, who apparently considered it necessary to keep on subjects familiar to her guest, spoke of England and described her visit in 1897 for the Diamond Jubilee.

'I remember,' she said, 'how we drove to Richmond in a carriage; I was quite a young girl, chaperoned by Maman. Ah, but it is a long time now. A little more tea, Mr Wilson? We Russians drink tea always. It is a poison, but we drink it all day.'

Charles declined her offer. By his side Irochka was scraping the remains of jam off her plate with a teaspoon. Although she made a considerable noise, no one seemed to notice her excessive appetite. There was a short silence, then Madame Leonidov turned to the girl who had come in with the cups and to whom no one had so far addressed a word.

'Maria Ivanovna, this afternoon you saw Madame Kondratieff?'

'Yes.'

'Oh, it is so sad. She is very ill and it is impossible to help her – there is no money.' She raised her shoulders. '*Que voulez-vous*? It is the same for us all.'

Charles felt embarrassed at the mention of their poverty. His fears had not been groundless. She was probably going to ask him to subscribe to some fund.

'What is the matter with her?' he said, hoping to divert this awkward topic.

'Oh, *tuberculose*. I don't know what you call it. Her husband is really too old to work, and she has a little son – the poor woman.'

There was another pause, which was broken by Homoutov, who had launched into one of his longest anecdotes about a certain General P. Unfortunately he was left to enjoy the story by himself, because Madame Leonidov was absorbed in her own thoughts and Charles was too embarrassed by the close scrutiny of Irochka, who, having at last finished her jam, turned to stare at the guest, to pay any attention to his rambling story. He watched a fly slowly crawling up his trousers and felt a disagreeable sensation at the back of his neck as though his collar had separated itself

24

from his shirt and would at any moment reveal a line of flesh above his coat. Just as his uneasiness at being silently examined by an inquisitive child grew intolerable, Madame Leonidov seemed to rouse herself, sent Irochka out of the room, and made a remark in Russian to the governess, who immediately rose to go. As she passed him, Charles looked at her. She was of average height, broad-shouldered and heavily built, but she carried herself with an easy grace which lent a certain charm to her figure. There was something arresting in her swaying walk and the poise of her well-shaped head. She turned at the door to speak to Madame Leonidov and Charles saw her pale face framed in heavy dark hair. She was not beautiful, but it struck Charles that there was some rare, appealing quality about her. She had hardly spoken since she came in, and the conversation at tea did not seem to affect her at all. She had sat there, quiet and aloof, and till that moment Charles had not even looked at her. Ordinarily he would not have noticed the silence of one woman, or the talkativeness of another. He was always absentminded, and his wife had never been able to train him in the art of handing cups and building up a fragile edifice of talk about nothing, necessary at all social functions in Bayswater and Golders Green. But this afternoon he was in a nervous, agitated state of mind rarely experienced by him, and which made him aware of facts to which otherwise he would have been wholly indifferent. He had always abhorred anything 'out of the ordinary', avoiding all the range of ideas labelled by him as 'unnatural', all the class of things which went into the category of 'foreign' and 'strange'. So that for him to feel what he immediately defined as the 'mysteriousness' of the silent governess was an unwonted but – he was surprised to find – not an altogether disagreeable sensation. He wondered why she stood – rather dramatically it seemed to him – with her hands clasped and her head upraised so that the light made a triangular shadow under her chin and down her throat. He started when the door closed quietly behind her. As though she had guessed the trend of his thoughts, Madame Leonidov said :

'You must think us Russians very different from the English. All this . . .' She made a circular movement with her hand as if including the disorder of the room into the meaning of her remark. 'But we are very *sans gêne* – I don't know how you call it.'

'Without convention,'suggested Homoutov.

'Ah, yes, that is it. We Russians, we have always liked to have freedom; we do not mind anything; and we like to see our friends always, even when our life is so different now. You understand me?'

She sighed. Charles muttered something which was evidently lost on her, because without answering she said to Homoutov:

'Pavel Andreivitch, you and your friend will have supper with us? You know how it is – just what we have in the house.'

'I am afraid . . .' Charles interposed hastily, lest he should find himself forced to prolong a visit too long already. Fortunately, Homoutov, too, refused.

'No, not this time, Elena Michailovna, if you forgive us. You know what it is to travel. I have so much to do before I leave Malta. I regret, but I must run away.'

Madame Leonidov was very gracious; she seemed unaware of the uneasiness of her English guest. She pressed him to come again, to remember that she would always be delighted.

'If you don't mind the simple ways here, because we are always glad to see our friends. You will come again, yes? – Just for a cup of tea?'

Charles assured her that he would like nothing better, and dived for his hat, which was under a chair, probably owing to Irochka's playfulness. The bearded individual followed them out, talking in Russian with extreme rapidity and many gestures. He had a humble, rather gushing manner, which accorded ill with the taciturn expression on his face when he was not speaking. He completely ignored Charles – perhaps because he knew no English.

It was already past seven and the sun was low over the harbour. They went down the steep path in silence, for the uneven wooden steps demanded all their concentration. When they had shut behind them the low gate which squeaked on its rusty hinges, Charles asked:

'Who is the man with the beard?'

'Abramovitch? He is a Jew and a doctor. A funny fellow, but kind-hearted, really. He lived with the Leonidovs even before the husband's death. You see, Madame Leonidov thinks she is ill and needs a doctor. Just a rich woman's fancy, you know; there's nothing in it.'

'Rich? – but I thought . . .'

Homoutov laughed in a peculiar affected way meant to convey sarcasm.

'Yes, I know, but she is a clever woman, and her husband, too, knew what to do with money. People say she has

27

capital invested in Switzerland; and besides, Malta is a very cheap place.'

For a while they walked on in silence; then Homoutov said:

'Abramovitch does not add much to her expenses. He would not leave, even if she wanted him to; he has followed her everywhere for years. He was always with them, even when the husband was alive. Poor fellow, none of us know much about him – he is very quiet; but of course people always talk.' He shrugged his shoulders.

They separated in the Strada Reale. Homoutov left him with a parting jest about the beauty of Maltese women and the infectious South. Charles watched him disappear down a side street – a dapper little figure with a sauntering gait, his cane swinging violently in all directions. It was a good thing, really, that he was leaving Malta. One couldn't be for long in the society of these perplexing foreigners. It was too unsettling, and above all things Charles hated being unsettled.

II

CHARLES HAD NOT INTENDED to go again to the Villa
San Michele, but he did, because he soon wearied of the
dullness of Valletta with its crowds of English visitors, its
narrow precipitous streets, where the way was so often
blocked by herds of goats or troops of clamouring, ragged
children. He hated the atmosphere of Southern laziness
which no British aggression could dispel; but he was equally
irritated by the English goods in shop windows and all the
traces of English life which he saw lurking everywhere, in
complete disharmony with Maltese surroundings. It was
consequently with a feeling of relief that he might at last
escape from his own boredom, that he climbed the steep
path to the villa.

No one seemed surprised to see him, and Madame
Leonidov was, as he put it to himself, 'all over him'. She
talked with a vivacity which surprised him, and begged him
to stay to supper.

'It is all so simple, but perhaps you will not mind. We
ask our friends to share what there is. You know that for
us poor exiles . . .' She made a gesture of apology and resig-

nation, 'But you will stay to do us pleasure. Here we are so far away from everybody.'

Charles stayed. He spent the time which separated an early tea from a late supper in an uncomfortable chair which creaked at his slightest movements. But Madame Leonidov talked to him and he was fascinated. He realised that she was older than he had thought at first. When she could not avoid the full glare of light on her face he saw that it bore carefully concealed marks of age. There were lines round her mouth, and the tell-tale fullness of her chin was disguised by the high, old-fashioned collar which supported her throat. Hearing her talk, however, he forgot all these things. He was pleased with the deliberate, emphatic way in which she made the most trivial and unimportant remarks. Her voice, low and caressing, rolled over him like wave after wave of sunlit water. She spoke with a kind of lilt inter-rupted only by pauses when she stumbled over an unfamil-iar English word. Charles felt as if someone were rocking him to sleep. He even had to stifle an occasional yawn. An unexpected sensation of comfort and security stole over him, breaking his resolve not to be pleased with anything. By nature restless and discontented, he was a man who felt acutely the lesser injuries of life. He was usually irritated with himself and everyone he had to deal with. From the time when he had been the dirtiest and most stupid boy in the lowest of the fifths, he had been conscious of his medi-ocrity.

'Charles, what a fool you are!' his wife would say, even when there was no need. And in his mind he always retorted:

'I know I am, and that is the worst of it: I can't even deceive myself.'

He perpetually tossed on the horns of the dilemma whether he was better than he seemed, or whether it could be possible that he seemed better than he was. To seem better was his secret longing. Preoccupation with his own self had soured his temper, and his deep-rooted ungovernable shyness spoilt his nerves. He was afraid to appear ridiculous, and consequently he never obeyed the more generous impulses of his nature. After all, what was the good, when people were sure to think him a fool?

Talking to Madame Leonidov he enjoyed a complete absence of self-consciousness. He did not often feel at ease; but somehow this woman with her leisurely movements and rich, mellifluous voice, soothed him and set his mind at rest about all the trivial anxieties which usually agitated it like flies swarming round a piece of meat. He felt that even if crowds of people came in and sat round in all the rickety chairs which in a haphazard fashion furnished the room, he would still retain his new and pleasant composure. Turning these thoughts over in his mind, he answered her almost at random. – Yes, he was in the Merchant Service. No, he had never been in America, didn't want to go, either; he was here on sick leave, the weather was so bad in England at this time of the year that he . . . His mind wandered – dysentery, England, Lucy – what was he saying? . . . Oh, yes, she was asking whether he did not already feel better in these lovely spring days. With a smile (he caught its reflection in a mirror and was pleased with it) he replied that at the Villa San Michele he felt perfectly well. He then told her of the weakness and apathy that still clung to him as a result of his long illness. Her unaffected concern for his health flattered him. He was ready to admit wholeheartedly that she was a charming, a delightful woman.

At supper he ate with relish and even found that tea without milk had quite a nice flavour. Abramovitch, too, seemed quite pleasant and Maria Ivanovna attracted him again by her silence. For the first time he met women who were not always chattering. He loathed the cackle with which the ladies of Lucy's acquaintance bridged the gulf of their stupidity; they were all foolish, over-dressed creatures, destined in a very few years to become stout malicious scandalmongers. He stayed long enough to hear Madame Leonidov play on the piano whose yellowish keys rattled when they were struck. She played by the light of two guttering candles, swaying gently to the rhythm of the music, so that her shadow leaped in grotesque strides up the wall and across the ceiling. Her playing was facile, smooth and even like her voice, with a cloying sweetness in it which pleased Charles, who secretly loved the sensuous rhythms of Chopin's melodies. (Of course, he never admitted a taste which, in these days when Bach was the rage, might have been condemned as mawkish.) Not content with nocturnes, and a waltz played with a lingering rubato, Charles begged for more. She played Brahms, and Abramovitch kept time with his feet, and fingers drumming on his knees. It was all, he decided, very nice and homelike. He knew quite well that this was not like any home that he had ever known, but the word suited his mood. When he left, his promises to come again were sincere. On the way back to his rooms he told himself that Russians were really very pleasant people, so free, so easy-going; there was nothing unnatural about them, no swank or false modesty, quite delightful. He must write and tell Lucy . . . no, he wouldn't – she was stupid and couldn't understand things.

From that day his visits became more and more frequent. He soon dropped into the habit of spending long hours at the Villa. He would wander into the drawing-room, and if there was no one there play tunes that he remembered from lessons at school on the old piano. Sometimes, if Madame Leonidov was reported to be unwell, it was Abramovitch who appeared, heralded by a faint rattling of pebbles with which he always filled his pockets. He spent most of his time in studying geology, and these were specimens he carried about with him and which had earned him the nickname of 'rattlesnake'. Sometimes it was Maria Ivanovna. She came rarely, and when she did she sat by the window and sewed. Although she hardly ever spoke to him, he liked watching her hands and the line of her neck half hidden by the thick coil of her heavy dark hair. She never looked up from her work. He learnt to wait for the fall of the pins which she dropped into a box by her side and which alone broke the silence in the room.

Gradually the atmosphere which reigned in the house absorbed him. He grew accustomed to irregular meals prepared by Maria Ivanovna with Abramovitch's help. He learnt that nothing was expected of him, that he could come and go as he pleased, that no one was sufficiently interested in him to criticise or blame anything he did. The fact of his presence was accepted without astonishment, as the most natural thing in the world.

One day, finding the drawing-room empty, he had gone out into the garden. A moment later he heard Madame Leonidov's voice at the window –

'Marie, who is that in the garden?' and she had answered:

'Oh, that is Mr Wilson.' But neither of them had troubled to go out to him or call him. They had just left him to himself.

It was then that he realised that though they were pleased to see him, although Madame Leonidov treated him with the exuberance she lavished on everyone, although Maria Ivanovna smiled at him and Abramovitch was quite willing to discuss geology, he would not be missed if he stayed away. They had taken him into their midst with the tolerance they showed to everybody, but more they could not do. They were too absorbed in living their own life, in doing what seemed to be so little – preparing and eating many meals, drinking tea, talking. They talked a great deal, though they never indulged in meaningless casual chatter. Two of them could not be for one moment in the same room without beginning a long discussion. They talked, not because it was necessary to talk out of politeness, but because they seemed to enjoy it. It was that which lent them a certain unreality in his eyes, for it made him understand that they lived in the past, from which they had been cut off, and which they were for ever trying to recapture in their minds. The future held nothing for them; the present was a mechanical existence interesting only in so far as it could reflect the life from which they had been severed. A vain, a useless attempt perhaps; but was anything else possible in this quiet backwater whither they had been driven by misfortune? He read an inner meaning into all that surrounded them – their belongings, their furniture. The pale-faced miniatures in rows on the dusty mantelpiece, the carved box of painted wood so out of place on the cheap thin-legged table, the gilded icons in the dark corner by the door – all these old, treasured things were living reminders of a past about which Charles was certain only of this – that it was out of keeping with the present, with the ugly green of the distempered walls, and the shabby uncomfortable chairs.

Charles felt this the more that he had a peculiar fondness for knick-knacks. The small, usually valueless, but sometimes beautiful objects with which people adorn their rooms never failed to attract his attention. He liked the smoothness of ivory, the smell of wood, the luminous transparency of glass. Bright colours and intricate shapes gave him a satisfaction he never experienced when confronted with formal art. His sympathy for the patient Oriental craftsman made him acquire a multitude of those trifles which abound in Indian and Chinese markets. He brought them home with something of a collector's pride; but Lucy always locked them away in the cupboard with glass doors that stood between the two lace-curtained windows of their drawing-room, and referred to them as 'The things my husband brings back from the East – it's nice to have them, of course, but they do collect so much dust.'

Charles felt sorry for these people, who were really very

kind to him. Often when he was left to himself he would finger the miniatures, which greatly attracted him, and think of the sadness of their life. No wonder Abramovitch was taciturn and Maria Ivanovna silent. They had something to do trying to pretend that their existence in this old, neglected house, badly in need of repair, was all that they had ever known. He found that though he questioned them about that time which had followed the Revolution (he was not well-informed on that subject), they were strangely reluctant to talk about it. Even Madame Leonidov, who willingly dwelt on topics which affected her even to the extent of shedding tears, was silent on this. If ever Abramovitch began to make pessimistic remarks about Russia and Bolshevism she threw up her hands in indignation and begged him to spare her.

'How can you talk like that!' she would exclaim. 'I cannot bear it. Have we not suffered enough and do you still want to make us suffer?'

Having silenced him, she would wipe her eyes and turn again to her patience.

Charles was not the only visitor at the Villa. He often saw other Russians, who came there as to a convenient meeting-place, and to whom he could not extend the sympathy he felt for Madame Leonidov's household. On the whole they seemed to be a loose lot.

Some talked too much, making themselves conspicuous by their loud voices and unrestrained laughter; others were so obviously pathetic. They behaved as though they always expected people to be sorry for them, and paraded their poverty without any apparent sense of shame. With them

Charles felt uneasy, because he was afraid that he might have to lend them money. With the vociferous ones he was completely at a loss. The jokes he understood struck him as being positively indecent; those he did not caused him to feel that he was being left out of the conversation. He frequently found himself the butt of remarks which seemed to him ill-natured and unjust, about the English. They all thought that they had been treated unfairly in politics before the Revolution, and monstrously now when so many of them were refugees in British dominions.

'It's all very well,' he thought, 'for them to say we are heartless. Anyway we are not all out for what we can get.'

He felt that this explained these noisy people who all wanted something and never ceased talking about it. Money was what most of them were after – very natural, of course, but why shout about it? His susceptibility was frequently offended by their blatant candour. Two girls who came sometimes talked of their private life with an outspokenness which rivalled that of any society novel. They made Charles blush. He even asked Madame Leonidov if it was quite usual. She shrugged her shoulders.

'I know, but *que voulez-vous*? And they are of a good family. Their mother was with me at the "Institut" in St Petersburg.'

One afternoon a woman whom he knew and actively disliked came in with a long tale of woe. It was said that she had disposed of two husbands with dexterity and no scandal, and that although she rather ill-treated her son she was very kind-hearted and pleasant. She repulsed Charles by the brilliance of her complexion, the audacious redness of her

37

hair, and her incessant chatter. She talked as much as she could, and when she was silent her bright eyes roved from face to face, watching for a chance to break into the conversation. On this occasion she was accompanied by a tall, dark woman who proved to be English. The dexterous Madame Dandré, as she called herself after her first husband who was believed to be dead, lost no time in confiding to those present how hardly she had been treated by a cruel fate. The story was lost on Charles; but the Englishwoman, whose husband was apparently Russian, told him what had happened in a listless voice which sounded as though it came not from a human throat but from a muffled gramophone.

'You see,' she said, fixing him with her large beautiful eyes, 'Madame Dandré was invited to lunch on board one of the ships of the fleet, and as she had only one pair of shoes, which were worn out, she mended them with cardboard and string. She slipped getting into a *dghaisa* and got her feet so wet that when she went on board the captain took her into his cabin and made her take off her shoes to dry them. Of course he had to throw away the cardboard soles. It must have been most disconcerting.' Her mouth slid into a mirthless smile and she relapsed into a silence from which no one tried to rouse her.

Charles watched the bright-haired sufferer with growing animosity. Her voice was as shrill as her laugh. Her parted lips revealed long uneven teeth which seemed the only real things in the featureless mask of her face. He noticed that a gold tooth showed at the corner of her mouth, and he experienced a feeling of disgust, as though he had inadvertently stepped on a slimy, repulsive animal. He sat in glum silence, nursing his rancour against this woman, until someone suggested that they should go into the garden. It was so lovely now; a pity to stay indoors. He made towards the door as though to follow them, but changed his mind and came back to his chair by the window. He could hear the women twittering outside. There was a bowl of purple anemones with large glazed petals and hairy stalks on a small table beside him. Obeying an impulse to indulge his feeling of annoyance, he pulled out a flower and one by one tore off its petals. He did not even notice that someone had come into the room. Suddenly he heard Maria Ivanovna's voice.

'You like flowers, Mr Wilson?' She was standing by the window, one hand on the faded green curtains. He looked at the mutilated thing in his hands. The leaves already had a faded, ragged look, as though they had been a long time without water. He felt embarrassed, like someone caught in a mean, cowardly action.

'Yes,' he replied, replacing the dismembered stalk in the bowl.

'I am afraid you have had a very dull afternoon,' she continued with a frank, pleasant smile. 'You don't like Madame Dandré and her friends.'

Charles protested. 'But I don't know them . . . I . . . I am sure they are very pleasant.'

She did not answer, but busied herself with the anemones, some of which had fallen out of the bowl on the table. When she looked up there was something cold and defiant in the expression of her eyes.

'Mr Wilson, why do you come here?' she said with a hard note he had never heard before in her voice. He was so surprised that for a moment he could not answer. What a question! He had never thought about it. Besides, wasn't it natural? Surely he could come if he liked without having a particular reason for so doing.

'I really don't know,' he said at last, hating himself for having been so obviously taken aback. 'But why do you ask?' He was going to add, 'Don't you like my coming?' but did not, feeling that such a personal question would only involve him in further difficulties.

'Because I thought you would know,' she replied without hesitating, and he had to look at her face to see if she was laughing at him. But it had the same passive, wistful look as ever. He thought that she was about to say something else, but she only picked up the anemones in their chipped white bowl and left the room.

Charles took out his spectacles and began to polish them with his handkerchief, as he always did when he was puzzled or annoyed. What an absurd conversation, he thought. Had she been rude or sincere in her questions? And if she had not meant to be rude, why was she so serious about it? After all, it could not matter to her, very much, whether he came or not! Many visitors came to the Villa, and because she was not often in the drawing-room she had very little to do with them. And then he was Madame Leonidov's guest, not hers. He felt that his confidence in these Russians had been severely shaken this afternoon. There was that red-haired cat – although she, of course, was not worth a single thought; but this girl, too, who had seemed so quiet and pleasant, could apparently behave very oddly. He thought of the dark-eyed Englishwoman with the dull voice. She would never have spoken like that. It struck him that perhaps they were all wondering at his frequent visits. The idea made him feel uncomfortably hot. Obviously her remark was a hint that he wasn't wanted. It served him right for being such a fool and mixing himself up with foreigners. One never knew where one was with them. Better to steer clear of them altogether. He would go away now and not come back. It would serve them right if they thought they would get something out of him. He got up and went to the window to see if Madame Leonidov was still in the garden – he supposed he would have to say goodbye to her. But both she and her guests had disappeared. Only Maria Ivanovna was slowly wandering up and down the path along the hedge of acacia and syringa bushes. So this was the last time he would see her. Although he was still angry, this thought made his heart contract with a sudden sense of loss. There was something about her that attracted him more than he would acknowledge to himself. He liked watching her sit, aloof and silent, in the drawing-room; he liked listening to her quiet low voice when she spoke, he liked the rare smile which sometimes crept over her face like a fugitive gleam of light across still water. He saw her turn a corner and disappear out of his sight. An early butterfly, with wings almost colourless, brushed against his face. He turned away from the window, determined to escape while no one was about.

As he walked through the garden he told himself sharply that he was a fool for bothering about 'these foreigners'. A stranger he was, and a stranger he would remain, involving himself in no difficulties, taking no risks. At the gate he almost ran into a woman who was coming up the road. They both pulled up sharply and he recognised her. It was too late to pass her without speaking. He had met her several times lately. She had coarse features and ugly red hands. Although she was always very amiable he disliked her. He felt her bright, inquisitive eyes rest on his face as she said, 'Good afternoon. Madame Leonidov is at home?'

'Yes.'

'And you are going so early!' The bright eyes had taken in his confused look.

'There are other guests there; goodbye.'

He raised his hat and went on. Unpleasant woman! Just his luck to run into her when he wanted to escape without being noticed.

III

FOR OVER A WEEK Charles stayed away from the Villa. He spent his time lazing about the harbour and wandering in and out of the foodshops where he took his meals. In a casual fashion he was interested in what he saw of the life of a town where so many civilizations had left their mark; but as he had little inclination to observe, and could not fall at will into the gently philosophical mood which in the educated and intelligent often takes the place of boredom, he was frankly bored. He tried excursions into the heart of the island, but that soon palled. He had a like aversion for sight-seeing and crowds – and Malta was at that season of the year crowded with foreigners. Gradually he learnt to distinguish the Russians from the throngs of Italians, English and French. He knew the men by their stoutness (almost without exception, those over thirty inclined to obesity) and their ill-fitting clothes; the women by the strained look their faces wore under the disguise of cosmetics. He had noticed that look of passive but stubborn resistance in Maria Ivanovna. He still felt nettled at the thought of her. He felt as if he had received a snubbing from someone whom he had expected to be always quiet and retiring, and he brooded over the galling incident, trying to explain to himself the waywardness of this strange girl. He now remembered another occasion when she had again lost the restraint which usually guarded her least actions.

It was one evening when he had stayed late listening to Madame Leonidov's endless talk about herself and her country. Vividly he recalled the semi-darkness of the room lighted by the only lamp, which had been placed on a stool by the side of Maria Ivanovna – engaged as usual in mending clothes. Again he saw the round patch of yellow light it made at her feet, and the ragged shadows in the corner where Abramovitch, his legs tucked under his chair, was tuning a guitar. The metallic twang of the bass string accompanied Madame Leonidov's talk like a remonstrating voice. When the light fell on it, his high, retreating forehead shone like polished ivory. Charles remembered all these details, although at the time he had only been an observer and had formed no part in the picture. That evening Madame Leonidov had been eloquent. Her pale eyes had gleamed when she had spoken of her beloved country. She had lingered over the description of its dreaming forests and snow-covered fields. (She had even quoted her own translation of some poem which talked a great deal about the moon and a snowstorm; but Charles had not understood it very well.) Her voice had risen and fallen in memory of the rapturous cadences of some forgotten nightingale. She had in fact for some hours been what the sympathetic would have called 'inspired', and the unkind 'loquacious'. Charles had enjoyed listening to her, not because he greatly cared for nightingales and snowstorms in the more distant parts of Europe, but because her voice, although it was now familiar, had never lost its fascination for him. When she spoke he felt as if he were being stroked by a large soft hand. He was suddenly jerked out of his somnolence by the harsh scraping of a chair. Maria Ivanovna had risen, and trailing some garments after her, walked towards the door.

'You are not going, Maria?' Madame Leonidov's voice almost gurgled with tenderness for the girl whom in moments of enthusiasm she would call her 'dear, adopted daughter.'

'Yes, I am tired of this; we hear it so often.'

As the door shut behind her, the guitar broke into a tune. Abramovitch's long fingers swept the strings with sudden energy, making plaintive sounds which reverberated in the silence. After what she had probably judged to be a suitable interval, Madame Leonidov remarked:

'I am afraid she does not care for our country. She feels not her exile.' And shaking her head she added as though someone had contradicted her: 'Oh, no, not at all. Perhaps she was too young to understand, too young.'

It surprised Charles that he should thus search his memory for an explanation of Maria Ivanovna's behaviour. It was so unlike him to ponder other people's actions that he saw in this a return of the nervous restlessness which had followed his long illness, and from which he had thought himself freed through the benign influence of the Russians at the Villa. Determined not to give way to weakmindedness, he shook off his preoccupation. After all, there was nothing extraordinary about that girl. Perhaps she was bad-tempered, but so were a good many people. He did not credit himself with insight into character, or an active imagination. Safety was the aim of his life, and he got that by taking no more notice of people than they did of him. Lately, it is true, he had experienced vague doubts about himself and longings for a somewhat bolder ideal, but he had shut his mind to them, resolved to keep to the straight and narrow way of security. What was the good of fighting against circumstances that had made him what he was?

Comforted by reflections of that nature, he decided to call again at the Villa. Madame Leonidov, who had always been so kind, probably resented the suddenness of his departure the last time he had been there. He really must try to conciliate her. He would go tomorrow and take her some flowers.

The next day being a Sunday he set off flowerless. He walked quickly up towards Floriana – the district outside Valletta where stood the Villa San Michele – and climbed the winding path through the garden with a sensation of pleasure. It seemed a long time since he had been there. The wistaria over the door was covered with flat purple flowers. Someone was standing at the drawing-room window. When he came nearer (his short-sightedness always annoyed him) he saw that it was Maria Ivanovna with an apron round her waist and bare arms reddened below the elbow by hot water. She greeted him first.

'Good morning, Mr Wilson. It is a long time since you have been to see us.'

'Yes, I am afraid so. But where are the others?'

'Oh, they have gone to church. It is Lent, you know.'

Somehow he had never imagined that Russians went to church on Sunday mornings like the rest of the world. A book he once read fostered the idea in his mind that their religion (when they had any at all) was a form of nature-worship. He remembered that it had said a lot about spirits and traditional superstition. His face must have shown his surprise, because she explained:

'You see, we have a small church in Sliema where we all go. It is only a room, and too small really, now that there are so many Russians in Malta.'

'And do you prefer to stay at home?'

'Well, there is the dinner to cook. A woman does it sometimes, but today there are going to be some guests, I believe . . . But of course you must not go . . .' she added, because Charles had already seized his hat which he had placed on the window-sill. 'Madame Leonidov will be delighted to see you – only you must not mind being by yourself while I am in the kitchen. They will come back quite soon now, I think!'

'Oh, you must let me help you. I am awfully good!' A vision of himself at home early in the morning flashed through his mind. He saw himself in stockinged feet fidget-ing over the gas stove on which the bacon would not cook. Lucy, who liked an extra half hour in bed, sometimes made him get up and prepare the breakfast. What was the good of having a husband home on leave if he could not make him-self useful?

'Certainly, if you like,' said Maria Ivanovna's voice. 'You can peel the potatoes!'

She let him in through the back door. The kitchen was

small and stuffy. Flies were buzzing round a piece of meat left on the table, and a tap dripped in the corner. All this struck him as another proof of the difference which existed between himself and these people. Even he could see that the floor had not been scrubbed for several days. Their ways were slovenly. Maria Ivanovna, who was bending over the small stove, seemed unaware that too much of her white underclothing showed at the neck of her blouse and that the hem of her skirt was undone. Charles felt pleased with the scrupulous neatness of his own clothes. He was wearing a discreetly striped tie which he felt added distinction to his appearance. He glowed with immaculate freshness, from the polished toes of his boots to the last wisp of his well-brushed hair.

Wrapped in an apron which was not clean, he peeled potatoes under Maria Ivanovna's gaze. He was more clumsy than useful, and she laughed at his efforts with a knife completely innocent of a sharp edge. It did not annoy him that she should be amused at his expense. He was pleased that she should see his willingness to conform to their habits. His pity for them only increased his sense of superiority; and his fear that they should become aware of it made him anxious to fall in with their ways.

He found it difficult to reconcile his mind, well-stiffened by regularity, to a casual existence. Although he admired the profound calm with which they avoided the fuss that Lucy, for instance, would have made over what he called 'little things', he could hardly imitate it. In fact, he could not decide whether it was praiseworthy or merely the sign of a complete indifference to all principles of order and stability.

Gradually, however, he forgot these thoughts in the pleasure of watching Maria Ivanovna move about the kitchen. He made the startling discovery that it was her presence he had missed during all the time when he had not been to see them. Had he been in the habit of using such words in connection with his own self, he might have said that she fascinated him as no other woman – not even the beautiful Madame Leonidov – had ever done. There was something so satisfying about the intangible grace of her movements; there was an indescribable, elusive beauty about her calm, sad face with its straight brows and high, pale forehead. The poise of her head, the coil of dark hair she wore low on the nape of her neck, stirred him with vague half-conscious delight. Her habitual silence, her independence appealed to him. She seemed completely unaware of the necessity of forming any ties with people whom, like Charles himself, she knew only because she frequently sat with them in the same room, shook hands with them, gave them tea, or told them in her low grave voice that Madame Leonidov was unwell and asked them to excuse her – but of course they would entertain themselves and not go before supper.

He had heard her do it often; had often watched her coming back from walks with Irochka; had seen her sitting by the window with a book she was not reading on her lap; but never before had he realised the importance of her person in the setting of the green walls, the unframed portrait of the stout ancestor over the mantelpiece, and the thousand and one objects jostling each other in that room which preserved so well the peaceful melancholy of the past.

As he looked at her now, he felt as if he had known her all his life. That gesture when she pushed up the hair which lay heavily on her neck was surely familiar; and so was the little smile which would glide unexpectedly over her still features. He had seen it often enough, but at this moment it seemed to him a revelation of her kind nature. Perhaps he had misjudged her. He felt sure now that she had all those rare qualities which made companionship pleasant and friendship invaluable. He had always been friendless, but he had the idea which men cherish when they are either very solitary or very companionable, that friends are among the best gifts of life. His desire for companionship was growing in the society of these Russians, for, whatever they lacked, they seemed to have the strange power of drawing people to themselves.

Maria Ivanovna stopped beating eggs.

'Well,' she said, 'how much have you done?'

There were only a few square-shaped potatoes in the basin he held on his knee.

'You are not very good; but I expect it will be enough.'

A moment later she spoke again, and he was so surprised at what she said that her words reached him as though they had been carried not by hers, but by another and unknown voice.

'I hope you were not angry at what I said the other day. Is it because of that you have not been here since then?'

His first sensation was one of disappointment because this remark seemed at variance with the idea he had only so recently formed of her. He had not expected that she would try to propitiate him and so suddenly break through the

aloofness which had hitherto surrounded her. He felt perplexed.

'Oh, not at all,' he muttered.

'I asked you,' she continued, 'because I often wondered
about it. People come here for such different reasons – Russians to exchange news or get a meal, and the English to
look at us. They never really like our ways, but they are
interested in us because if they are intelligent they think
they may learn from us; if they are not, they can flatter
themselves that they are so much cleverer and richer than
we are.'

'Oh, but I assure you I came out of curiosity only, the
first time, and even then not altogether, because I came to
please Homoutov. After that I came because I liked to.' She
seemed amused – in fact during the whole of their conversation he felt as though she were mocking him a little.

'I have often seen you look quite bewildered among us
all, as though you were not sure what would happen next.
Confess that when you sit on the sofa you often think of
those cobwebs just over your head? . . . The woman who
comes in will never sweep them away,' she added in a matter-of-fact voice, as though her mind were wholly occupied
with the thought of the cobwebs and the dirty handsome
Maltese who sometimes idled in the kitchen and always
slipped away early to the lover who whistled to her by the
kitchen door. Out of the drawing-room windows they would
often see the blue shawl she wore on her head moving in
jerks along the garden wall, and Madame Leonidov never
failed to make some remark about the Southern temperament and the difficulties of having a Maltese servant.

'I think you are wonderful,' he answered, looking at her smiling, animated face, and directly he had said this wondered whether he meant her alone, or all the others too. She did not appear to notice the ambiguity.

'Oh, but we are not. Why do you say that? . . . Because we talk a great deal about what we used to be? Our exile has made us very sentimental, I am afraid. But there is nothing for people like us to do. Every day is the same as the last. There is no other work for us but to remain alive. Besides, so few of us know how to work. We think we are very clever and what you English call "artistic", but that is all. We have a reputation for being strange and gifted, but there are not many of us who are honest enough to know that it is a false reputation. After all, we get much by it.'

'You are very bitter,' he said, wondering what made her talk like that.

'Bitter? No, only just. But perhaps you are right. Justice is often bitter because life . . .' She paused as if anxious to save herself from a platitude. Charles made an attempt at a complimentary remark:

'Of course, I don't know what you think about yourselves, but to an ordinary Englishman you seem awfully nice.' A poor effort, but he had never been good at that sort of thing. She made no reply.

At that moment voices reached them from the garden. Evidently Madame Leonidov had returned. Irochka, in white, with her straight yellow hair flapping down her back, rushed past the open kitchen window and burst in through the door with a loud cry of –

'Mashenka! Mashenka!' (she frequently called Maria Ivanovna that).

52

Seeing Charles she stopped short, sniggered, and ran out again, banging the door behind her. He checked the impulse to say 'awful child!' and only remarked:

'Rather spoilt, isn't she?'

'Sh-sh!' came from Maria Ivanovna, and looking up Charles saw Madame Leonidov's face at the window. He remembered that he was still in the dirty apron and tried to untie the strings but in his embarrassment only succeeded in twisting them into inextricable knots. There was nothing to do but come up to her as he was, and, wrapped in the offending garment, take her outstretched hand. Although she was smiling, it seemed to him that her voice sounded cold and displeased.

'Ah . . . Mr Wilsonn! . . . It is so kind of you to help. I thought you had already forgot us. It is quite a long time since you have come to the Villa. You will stay to lunch with us, yes? Maria Ivanovna needs you no longer now. You must come out into the garden.' There was the same cold gleam, unwarmed by the light of the sun, in her hair and eyes.

He got rid of the apron and went out. The sunlight was dazzling. The walls of the house looked white against the purple flowers of the wistaria, and in the shadows of the trees the patches of white convolvulus seemed like the last traces of melting snow. Under the drawing-room windows Madame Leonidov was talking to her guests. One was the Bernini girl whom he had met outside the gate on the day of his flight from Maria Ivanovna, and who, as usual, wore mustard-coloured stockings and a coat tight for her under the arms and across the shoulder blades. The other was a pale little woman in a red hat too bright for her thin-featured bird-like face. A man was with them – tall, tightly buttoned into a brown suit, with dark sleek hair and dark eyes half-hidden under heavy eyelids. His long nose hooked down to full mobile nostrils, and a thick upper lip thrust out above the lower emphasised the look of cunning arrogance on his sallow face.

Madame Leonidov greeted Charles with a friendly gesture.

'Ah, Mr Wilsonn – at last. You know Mademoiselle Bernini, and this is Madame Joukovsky, a friend of my childhood.'

The little grasshopper (she reminded him of one because she sauntered when she walked) elongated her mouth into a smile and kept it there as though anxious that everyone should know how nice and pleasant she was. When Charles shook his large nerveless hand, the sallow individual ('Captain Bassanov, a great musician – he has promised to play to us this afternoon') raised his upper lip, revealing teeth set at large intervals in his gums. Charles noticed that when he spoke saliva gathered at the corners of his mouth. He knew very little English and his vocabulary consisted chiefly of 'Ah, that is so,' with a slight hiss over the 's', which letter he could not pronounce. The conversation languished. Madame Leonidov, in spite of her frequently expressed delight at having tethered a celebrity ('a man known to all the musical world, Mr Wilsonn') to herself for the afternoon, was apparently not in a good humour. She cut short a remark ventured by 'the grasshopper', and hustled them all indoors with undisguised impatience directly Maria Ivanovna had called out through the window that 'everything was ready.'

Lunch was a tedious affair because the celebrity had an excellent appetite and Madame Leonidov's energies were wholly concentrated on feeding him with the choicest morsels. Charles's aversion for the great man increased as he watched him eat with the voracious haste of an animal that expects to have his food snatched away.

'Brute!' he thought, following with his eyes the lightning movements of his fork. Evidently this was a man full of what Madame Leonidov called 'temperament'. He could not sit still. When everyone had settled down to the endless post-prandial tea-drinking he paced the room, talking with fiery volubility, his restless eyes sliding with a sideways look over the faces of the listeners. They received the sallies of his wit with exclamations of 'Ach, Ivan Alekseivitch!' and discreet laughter. The 'grasshopper', who was next to Charles, quite shrivelled up under the fire of his eloquence.

'Captain Bassanov is . . . how do you say it? . . . so *drôle*!' she explained, blushing a dull pink to the roots of her faded brown hair; for apparently the celebrity's humour was of that coarseness which Charles found it impossible to emulate. Although his timid nature shrank from it, he felt that it was proper to his sex, and would have given much not to he shocked by the candour which he knew to be indispensable in the higher circles of society. Most of what the sinister captain said was lost on him, however, and he was bored until Maria Ivanovna came in, followed by Abramovitch, and took a seat beside him. She made several remarks to him, while Madame Leonidov sailed over to the piano, and, having dusted the keys, cajoled the celebrity on to the piano stool.

'Captain Bassanov will now play to us,' she announced with the proud air of one who is personally responsible for the talent about to be revealed to the audience.

'It is such an honour that he will play in this little room, to so few people, but he knows that we love music!'

The great man passed a nervous hand through his hair, allowing a lock to fall over his forehead. Thus prepared for the strain of emotion, he bowed his head over the yellowed keys of the piano.

'*Il se recueille*,' breathed Madame Leonidov in a penetrating whisper.

As the first chords crashed through the room, Charles stifled a yawn. He disliked the intellectual effort of listening to 'high-brow' music, especially when it became a sort of futuristic cat-calling. Discordant noise irritated him profoundly.

When at last Bassanov had covered the full range of disharmony, Charles turned to Maria Ivanovna with a questioning look.

'Prokofieff,' she said under cover of the applause.

'Oh,' he replied, as though this explained everything; but it left him as ignorant as before. He had never heard of the man and did not wish to hear more. His ears were still tingling from the merciless noise which had been inflicted on him for a full half hour. Unfortunately it was on him that Madame Leonidov turned to express her enthusiasm.

'Is it not wonderful?' she said, anxious that no one should escape from paying their full tribute of praise. 'It is so full of life.'

'Yes, marvellous,' he muttered.

'It is such joy to me that in our exile there are still those who are *devoués* to Art. When I have this music in my soul I feel that our country is not to die. It is men like Captain Bassanov, who give all to an ideal, who will save us from this.' She raised one hand towards the ceiling. Charles looked round the room. Abramovitch, as usual in the farthest corner of the room, was examining an oblong brownish stone through his pocket magnifying glass. The 'grasshopper' seemed to have shrunk farther into her red extinguisher-like hat. The Bernini girl had turned her attention to the musician, who had recovered sufficiently to notice the eager glances of her lustrous black eyes. There was the slight feeling of unrest which comes over a room full of people when no one quite knows what is expected of them. Alone Maria Ivanovna seemed unconcerned with everything around her. Her eyes fixed on some distant object seen only by her, she was smiling a little and that faint smile softened the severity of her expression. He had never been close enough to her to notice the shadowy down on her upper lip and the hair which curled round her temples. Covertly he examined her face, surprised that he should suddenly find it beautiful, and realising that he derived a pleasure which nothing could mar or interrupt from her presence. As long as she sat there he felt that he could even listen to that ass making a fool of himself at the piano.

Thus slightingly did Charles reflect about the celebrity who, his sleek hair once more in place and a thin line of moisture on his lip, expounded his philosophy of art to the admiring Madame Leonidov.

IV

EVERYONE AT THE Villa San Michele soon guessed the new reason for Charles's frequent visits. The rumour that Madame Leonidov's latest conquest (for she had the reputation of being something of an angler) was paying attentions to Irochka's governess spread around the circle of her acquaintance with lightning rapidity. She herself admitted that 'Mr Wilsonn has taken it into his head to become interested in Maria,' and she never failed to add, '*Pauvre fille*, she is not at all pretty and so *stupide*. She has not an idea, really not one in her big head.' She would most often repeat this to Vera Bernini because she knew that Vera's tongue was what she called '*bien pendue*'. Dear Verochka never missed a chance of telling people what they might like to know, and she had such a charming way of putting things. People would frequently repeat her amusing remarks. Even Zvonkoff, who had such a reputation as a humorist, would refer to what Vera Antonovna had said about so-and-so. She had called him a . . . It was a *mot*. He himself could not have made a better. Yes, Verochka was good company for a lonely woman.

Meanwhile Charles himself was unaware of the curiosity he had roused at the Villa, for it was so slowly that he had grown conscious of the magnetic influence which drew him there. He was surprised when one day he had spent some time talking to Maria Ivanovna in the garden that Madame Leonidov had treated him coldly and been so very distant. He was at a loss how to account for this change in her. She either ignored him entirely or made remarks, which he realised were meant for him, but which he could never quite understand. They usually began with 'There are people . . .' and ended with a meaning look at Vera. To his annoyance she was very often there. She treated Madame Leonidov with fatuous adoration, flattered her, was always ready to obey her slightest whim, and never missed an opportunity of telling everyone, even Charles, although he could not follow her French, which was said to be an excellent imitation of Gallic vivacity, that she was a wonderful woman, so charitable, so kind! Charles thought that this Vera was a viper, and turned from the hostility, which he dimly felt in her and Madame Leonidov, to Maria Ivanovna. She was different from the others, with her quiet assurance and placidity. She gave Charles that sense of security which he had at first thought to find in Madame Leonidov and her friends. They had seemed such free, easy, uncritical people, but now with every day they grew more changeful and difficult to understand, each of them a prey to those dark thoughts and obscure emotions from which he had always fled.

Anything strange and unusual was always avoided by him. He was one of those to whom 'artist' and 'crank' are synonymous, not because he despised such people, but because he was afraid that any sympathy for them might drive him to share in their self-inflicted torment. After all, did one not have enough to suffer from life without thinking about it as they always did? Convinced that he was sufficiently burdened by all the uncertainties and vicissitudes which daily befell him, he shut his eyes to everything that was not immediately before them and only sought the company of those who would not be likely to disturb his equanimity. He had liked the Russians at the Villa, for with them he had lost his fear of seeming ridiculous because his hair always looked as though it had been crimped and because the only sensational incident of his past was his removal from a public school into the Merchant Service. But it was in Maria Ivanovna that he had at last found someone who did not expect much from him; who seemed content that he should be as he was, not good-looking, not well-educated, and who was nevertheless ready to give him her sympathy and her companionship. She was absolutely sincere; she did not seem haunted by doubts and misgivings. That quality which separated her from others was, as he now realised, a perfect serenity. This inward calm, which was constantly reflected in her ways, drew him strangely towards her, but at the same time it perplexed and baffled him. His growing intimacy with her did not lessen the sense of the mysterious, which he had felt about her even when he saw her for the first time. It remained unfathomable. He was, however, too pleased with her society to wonder much at her strangeness, except when apprehension seized him that he would lose her friendship and, with it, his newly found confidence in himself.

One day, towards the end of March, he came into the house through the kitchen (as was now his habit, because she was most often there) to find Vera, sitting on the table, engaged in telling some story, to which Maria Ivanovna listened with a look of concern on her face. They took no notice of him. Charles, who had by this time learnt a few words of Russian, understood something about a son, the English, and yellow flowers. As usual, the woman must be talking nonsense! He felt annoyed because he grudged others Maria Ivanovna's company, and besides Vera was so impossible. He hated her ugly red hands which bore the marks of chilblains, her sharp inquisitive eyes, always moving from side to side, her bold handsome face with its hooked nose and firm, pointed chin. He resented her intrusion in the kitchen the more when he knew he had no right to resent it. Hadn't he been told often enough that Vera and Maria Ivanovna were great friends? In the drawing-room Madame Leonidov and Abramovitch were playing cards. Irochka, quiet for once, was engaged in a game behind the window curtains, which at every movement made by her ruffled along the floor. Charles sat down and allowed himself to sink into gloomy reflection. Everything seemed cheerless. Madame Leonidov and Abramovitch were too busy with their whist to talk to him, even if he had wanted to make conversation. Why couldn't Maria Ivanovna come? What on earth was she doing in her kitchen with that cat in yellow stockings? Why suddenly should they have so much to say to each other? At last Madame Leonidov looked up from her cards.

'But where is Vera? Has she not finished telling Maria?'

'Telling her what?' said Charles.

'Oh, you have not heard? A terrible thing has happened to poor Vera. She is quite ill with anxiety, poor child. I cannot tell you. Let her come in here and relate it over again.'

Abramovitch struggled out of his chair and fetched Vera. She did not look very ill; on the contrary, she enjoyed rehearsing the tale she must already have told as often as she had found people to listen to her.

She told him (in French, as she always avoided speaking English) what he already knew; that, owing to difficulties which they all felt (Madame Leonidov sighed quietly), she had taken a situation as a companion to a lady who had two sons. She was English, and one of the sons used to spend part of the year with her in Malta. The story which followed this preamble was told with so much eloquence and such deep feeling that Charles only followed the drift of it.

It appeared that this son had arrived the other day a little unwell and nervous, Vera had thought, and yesterday he said (she had been using the sewing machine in the next room – that was how she knew) that he would spend the evening with a friend. He had not come back. They waited till the morning. Of course she couldn't leave the mother alone. In the morning he had been found by a workman climbing about on some scaffolding with a suitcase in his hand; he was quite mad. He had been taken straight to a hospital; poor boy, he was only twenty-two. 'And can you imagine,' she continued, 'what the mother did when she heard the news? She telephoned to the hospital to ask if the suitcase was safe. It was a new one, she told me. A new one! She did not ask about him. She thought only of the suitcase.

Oh, those English, they have no feelings; they have no heart. Can you imagine a Russian mother thinking about a suitcase when she heard that her son was mad? I wanted to shake her. I wanted to tell her that her heart ought to break. But she had an ordinary breakfast and then I had to take her dog for a walk. Oh, it is dreadful, dreadful! They don't know what has made him go mad, but he hates yellow colour. There was a yellow bedspread on his bed and he tore it to pieces. I took him some flowers this afternoon – of course I was very careful not to choose yellow flowers. Is it not terrible? I cannot stop asking myself why yellow, especially yellow, should affect him so much.'

'Something to do with her stockings,' thought Charles, and immediately felt sorry that he could not make the remark out loud. 'Why do you think the English are so heartless, Mademoiselle?' he asked her, when he had put the sentence into his halting French.

'Oh, everyone knows they are. Perhaps we have no self-control, but we have feelings and we show them.'

'Believe me, it is a matter of convention.' Charles started at the sound of Abramovitch's voice. It seemed a long time since he had heard him speak. 'The English convention is self-control; ours is – emotion. We foster tumultuous feelings, as they do their restraint. Their way is perhaps the best. Think for yourself, Vera Antonovna. Would you not rather take the dog for a walk than face a *crise nerveuse*?'

'But this is nonsense!' interrupted Madame Leonidov; 'you speak as if we were all hypocrites, as if all the emotion of our souls . . .'

'Elena Michailovna, I said nothing about your soul. I

only wished to convince Vera Antonovna that perhaps she misjudged the unfortunate mother and that the difference between Russian tears and English hard-heartedness is not as great as she thought. No, not great at all, just convention, my friend; a convention very dear to the human race.'

He relapsed once more into gloomy silence and began to stride about, rattling the stones in his pockets as he walked. Charles could hear him muttering to himself. He caught the words 'sincere', 'humanity', and smiled. Poor Abramovitch, his science did him little good! Soon after he rose to go. Madame Leonidov was talking to Vera, and Maria Ivanovna had disappeared again. He felt annoyed that he had not been able to speak with her and that he could not banish Vera's story from his mind. He thought the whole thing very stupid. What did the young ass want to go and make a fool of himself for? Drunk probably. Yellow flowers, indeed! just like that beastly girl to go mooning round him with flowers. He was sick of their sentimental talk. Vera and Madame Leonidov couldn't keep their 'emotions' (in his mind he stressed the word) to themselves. Abramovitch wasn't much better.

'I think I will walk with you to Valletta,' he heard the Jew say as he opened the door. 'I would like to go for a walk this evening. Elena Michailovna, you will excuse me. I will say goodnight now.' He kissed her hand and followed Charles.

It was a still, windless evening. The sunset had left a rift of green in the dark sky and thin, wandering clouds were gathered round the pale rim of the moon, which as yet scarcely showed above them.

Abramovitch pointed it out to Charles. He seemed anxious to talk this evening. He walked with long, uneven strides, his thin hair disordered so that Charles could see the bald patch on the top of his head. He never stopped making remarks which perhaps he himself thought unimportant, because he tried a new subject with every sentence. They had talked of the fine weather, the Mediterranean climate, of fishing in Sardinia and the geological features of the Maltese islands, when Abramovitch turned suddenly towards Charles and, taking his arm, said in a voice which sounded forced and nervous:

'Mr Wilson, I hope you will not think me impertinent. If you would look upon me as a friend, it would help me so much. I wanted to ask you . . . I think you like Maria Ivanovna: I have noticed it. Of course, I do not know what your intentions are, but if you . . .'

'My intentions? Great Heavens, man! I don't know what you are talking about. I . . . I haven't got any . . .'

His anger made him stammer over his words. He could not tell whether he was more annoyed at the foolishness of the notion or at the fact that others had discovered and were evidently talking about something of which he himself was not aware. Anyway, it was nothing to do with Abramovitch.

'Besides,' he added, anxious to put an end to the conversation, 'don't you know I am . . .?' He was going to say 'married'. He had quite forgotten that he had not spoken to them about his wife. There had been so little need to talk about himself and the thought of her had never come into his mind when he was at the Villa. But Abramovitch interrupted him. He had lost the self-control he had been praising earlier in the evening. Charles noticed that the hand he had laid on his sleeve was trembling and he spoke very fast.

'Mr Wilson, I beg your pardon. You must excuse me. I do not know why I spoke to you like that. I beg you to forget it and to consider me your friend. I did not wish to offend you. I do not know how to explain to you . . .'

The idea that perhaps Abramovitch himself had intentions flashed through Charles's mind. That he, a man old before his time, worn out, taciturn, so like what Charles himself with his weak eyes and fussy ways might be at fifty-five, should have enough life in his body to love a woman, and that woman Maria Ivanovna, was a ludicrous thought. His resentment vanished. He laughed.

'Oh, don't worry.' How pleasant and cheerful his voice sounded! 'Of course I understand. I like Maria Ivanovna. She is very interesting, like all Russians are to us.'

'So you think us interesting, as does everyone else? Yes, poor exiles, refugees, almost beggars that we are. We often have as much attention paid us, as if we were prosperous and important.'

They were now walking through the streets of Valletta, quiet at last, except for the occasional bark of a dog or the shutting of a window. The moon had broken through the clouds and hung low in the sky. It played with their moving shadows. Long and thin they bounded along the walls, curled round water pipes, shrunk into gutters. Charles thought of a fantastic procession of ghosts through a city dead with sleep.

Lately his imagination had preyed upon him. He could not keep at bay all the stray foolish thoughts, which would never have occurred to him before, and which now stirred in his mind; clumsy, half-formed children of that part of his being that he had always resolutely ignored.

Abramovitch started talking again. 'Mr Wilson, I should indeed like you to think of me as a friend. I have great respect and admiration for Maria Ivanovna, and you sympathise with Russians. You understand them, perhaps.'

Charles felt that he was being provoked into useless discussion and he answered lightly, as though he were only keeping up a conversation.

'Oh, I confess I have no ideas about it, but I think you are all admirable, the way you manage to live and keep together.'

These words that he had thought ordinary enough had the effect of an intoxicant on Abramovitch. He pushed his hand through his hair (this with him was a sign of great agitation) and stopped in front of Charles, so that he found himself with his back to a wall.

'Admirable? You think them admirable! So does everybody, but I tell you that they are not; that they are base and stupid and not worthy of admiration. All of them. I am not a Russian. I am a Jew, but I have served them all my life. All the years when I was young I worked for them, wearing myself out in their hospitals for their sick and their poor. Cholera in the villages, neurasthenia in the fashionable resorts; I have tended all the diseases of their degenerate bodies and I know the disease of their hearts. They have deceived you, as they deceive everybody. There is only dust and rottenness in their lives, just as there is dust on their icons and all the things that they keep round them. They are refugees; they have been driven out of their country; they have nothing and they seek nothing. They are content to hide themselves behind the thin walls of their weaknesses and superstitions. There they are secure – they are admired. Have you not noticed how passionately they cling to the old and clothe themselves with the worn out tatters of ten and twenty and thirty years ago? Oh, I am ready to admit that they have suffered, but are they any better for their poverty and their loss? I have always been an idealist, Mr Wilson. I have always believed in those things with which great men blind us to reality. Fool that I was. I thought that they would come out with new souls from the sudden wreck of all that was good and bad in their lives. I thought that their eyes would have been opened to their own worthlessness; that they would have learnt to stand together; although poor and defeated and unknown, at least together, to try to find some meaning and some purpose in a new life. But do you know what they have done instead? They have made of this new life a false image of the past, and, what is more, they have made the world believe in it. The Russian refugee is fashionable. Last year I was in England and in Paris. Everywhere I saw traces of that interest for all that is Russian: the Russian ballet aped in the music halls, Chekhov plays on the English stage, Russian tea-shops and everything *à la russe*. Vain fools, we think that we can give the world something new. We think that we have with us, that we have brought out from Russia, a secret vitality, the Russian spirit, which can be dealt out in carved wooden boxes and in glasses of vodka, sold at fashionable restaurants in Montmartre.

'Like madmen, we shout and quarrel about nothing. We deceive ourselves so much, that we can believe in our own importance and think that, besides us, no one else matters. We talk about our unity and our faith, but our priests quarrel so bitterly that they abuse each other in their own churches, and our generals call councils to decide questions of military etiquette. It's almost funny, isn't it? We have kept all our prejudices, even our old political ones. The same parties which once struggled for power abuse each other in the papers they publish at the expense of ignorant benefactors and . . .'

Charles tried to interrupt him. All this might be true, but he wasn't going to stand listening there all night.

'I know you don't believe me,' Abramovitch went on, ignoring him, 'but you would if you knew what I see every day. They treat each other like dear friends and cheat themselves into thinking that they are charitable and good, and that all the affection and kindness they show is sincere. But at heart they are as bad as they ever were: hypocrites and cowards and liars.'

They had wandered down towards the harbour. The moon, rising and falling in yellow smoke-coloured clouds which drifted like mist across the sky, threw patches of tarnished golden light on the sea. Charles sat down on a coil of rope. The water, lapping monotonously against the stones of the quay, had a familiar, slightly nauseating smell of stale oil and fish. He hardly listened to Abramovitch, whose voice throbbed, like a distant engine, in his ears. His angular high-shouldered figure looked fantastic in the moonlight. His long, flapping coat tails reminded Charles of a crow's wings when it beats them for the last time before its claws touch the ground. He was very tired and when he closed his eyes he saw Madame Leonidov, Vera, Maria Ivanovna, the sinister Bassanov even, all these people against whom Abramovitch seemed to have such a fierce grudge and whom only yesterday he had thought – yesterday, yesterday now seemed a long time ago – yesterday he had said to Maria Ivanovna that he did not like the moon – and there he was sitting in the moonlight. . . .

The voice which he had for the moment forgotten sounded again in his ears.

'Mr Wilson, I must ask you to forget all that I have said. It does not matter. When people talk as I have done tonight they always wish their words unsaid, or at least forgotten. And so they are, so they are,' he repeated as though he were trying to force these words into his own memory.

'We can remember so little, and we do not want to remember more. If we did, we might go mad, like that Englishman of Vera's. Who knows? Perhaps he remembered something which made him forget even the new suitcase, and his mother was quite right to think of it, because he could no longer do so himself.'

Suddenly he started walking away, and before Charles caught him up he had reached the top of the steps which led to the street. They parted hurriedly. Abramovitch seemed anxious to get home as quickly as possible.

Charles spent a restless night. He could not banish from his mind the smell of oil and fish which had crept in with him into his small, stuffy room.

V

IT WAS ONLY WHEN an insistent letter came from his wife
that Charles realised how soon he would have to leave
Malta. His leave would be up after Easter, which this year
fell early in April, and she demanded that he should come
home. Apparently she had been worried by his silence, even
to the extent of suggesting that she should join him for a
holiday. So like her, he thought, to make a holiday an excuse
for not leaving him alone. In February she could not have
dreamed of stirring from home, but at Easter she could
think of going even as far as Malta. Of course it was impossible that she should come. There was the expense, and
besides, almost against his will, he had grown to love this
strange, beautiful island, unlike anything else he had
known, and would not share its beauty with her, who would
not understand. With her incessant chatter and her curiosity she would make him hate the place. She would want to
go to the Naval Club and on board the battleships; she
would rush about with a guide book and at every minute
think she was being robbed. It would be like her to scream
if a street-vendor plucked her by the arm. She would be

more unbearable here than in Michael Mansions.

This sea-bounded, isolated corner of the South, midway between the aridity of the desert and the ordered, cultivated beauty of the French coast, had obliterated from his mind the bleak memories of his home. It travelled back to them with renewed aversion. The trees in the square opposite the tall, grey block of houses, known for some obscure reason as Michael Mansions, would by now be budding into dusty green. That little space, intersected by straight gravel paths, and bounded by tall railings, rust-brown from the rain and damp, would be full of children, perambulators and nurses. As he thought of it, it seemed to him that the whole of his and Lucy's lives lay between that square and the cake-shop at the corner, where the children stopped daily in greedy admiration of the piles of dry, pink cakes, and the tall, yellow bottles of Kia-ora lemon squash, displayed summer and winter in its windows. He would have to return and daily pace that street with the square and the cake-shop for his landmarks. He knew it would not be for long, but the days he would spend there seemed interminable in their dullness.

He wrote back saying that he longed to be at home again and would be back in a fortnight's time, travelling overland from Marseilles. When he posted the letter he felt as if he had deliberately and of his own will cut himself off from freedom. The word had only lately assumed importance in his vocabulary. He had indeed never been conscious of that power, which, sometimes interpreted as the highest ideal of mankind, had for him come to mean all that he had enjoyed in Malta: peace of mind, and the society of people who somehow fostered in him the pleasant realisation of his own importance. The Russians at the Villa, whatever Abramovitch had to say about their morals (and secretly Charles held the opinion that morals, like one's choice of food, were a private concern; and that those who censured them invariably belonged to that dangerous class of men with ideas and convictions), made him feel at ease; they had treated him with attention which flattered him, as a man who fears to seem ridiculous in the eyes of others is bound to be flattered. It was his misfortune that he was conscious of his own insignificance. He saw in himself the reflection of his mother's character, if the weak, pale-eyed woman that she had been could be credited with anything so positive. He had inherited his susceptibility and fussy ways from her. She was frightened and unresisting, so that she had not even had the strength of mind to survive her youngest child in spite of the dismay of her husband, who protested even by her bedside that she could not leave him to bring up four children by himself. She had left him, however, and Charles had cherished a tender, somewhat sentimental memory of her. He had been her favourite, and he felt that she was the only woman who had loved and understood him. But his recollection of her had not been sufficient to fill the void into which had stepped so unexpectedly the figure of Maria Ivanovna. That sort of intimacy had grown up between them which is unmarred by the disappointments and longings of love, and which either precedes it or follows after when passion has already spent itself. He had never wondered whether he loved her, but now, when he knew that he would soon have to leave her and relinquish all those sensations of peace and well-being that he had experienced in her company, he felt regret more poignant than he had ever known. It was akin to that feeling which visits even the most reasonable and clear-headed men, when they are forced to leave that which by its familiarity has become dear to them, and for which they have never sufficiently cared until that moment when they realise that they will be separated from it, perhaps for ever. His heart contracted with pain when he thought of the Villa.

That house with its neglected garden still prodigal of flowers seemed to him now a sort of little paradise, secluded and carefully walled in from the outside world. He asked no better than that he should spend all his life there: sitting in the cool, semi-darkness of the drawing-room listening to the flick of Madame Leonidov's cards on the table, watching the ray of dust-laden iridescent light, which filtered through the half-closed shutters, creep across the floor and in a long zigzag up the wall. He saw it all now as though it already belonged to the past, and were already out of his reach, driven away from him by the spectre of the drudging life of Bayswater.

Unable to shake off his depression, Charles wandered up to the Villa. The oleanders were in bloom, and the flowering bougainvillea shed a deep purple glow over the wall to which it clung. As if on purpose, everything seemed especially beautiful and excited his resentment.

Several guests were already in the drawing-room when he arrived, and he found them discussing the approach of Easter and an important service which was to take place on the next Sunday. He was given a hurried explanation of this by Abramovitch, who appeared in trousers of a sea-weed green, before going out in search of geological specimens. He could not tell them now that he was going away; he would wait till Maria Ivanovna came in. He was glad when at last she did come, because her smile and a glance from her eyes were enough to banish his restlessness and make him forget his cares. He seized the first opportunity of drawing her aside.

'You know,' he said hurriedly, as if afraid that she would escape before he had had time to tell her what was on his mind, 'you know, I am going away very soon.' He tried to see her face, because directly he had spoken it had seemed to him that she was on purpose turning her head away, but she looked round, and he became painfully aware of the calm, undisturbed expression on her face.

'I suppose your leave is over. I am sorry. Madame Leonidov hoped that you would he here for our Russian Easter.' Charles was disappointed. He had hoped that she would find better words than these in which to accept the fact of his going. Had there been no tie of friendship between them? After all, he did not expect her gratitude for his admiration (it was the first time he used such a word about her), but only that she should allow her voice, her eyes to betray something of the regret which she ought to share with him. But she was quite silent, and seemed preoccupied only with what Irochka was doing in the garden. They remained standing side by side, and he pulled aside the curtain, which obscured her view into that corner where Irochka's white frock was just visible behind a clump of jessamine. He was deeply hurt by her indifference.

Abramovitch had said that their hearts were cold. Could it be true of her, who, he had thought, possessed a rare and sensitive nature, incapable of grudging sympathy? He would have stood there all the afternoon, brooding over his wrongs, had not Madame Leonidov called out to him.

'Mr Wilson, you must come and have tea now. You have not found the time amusing? I am sorry; we have been talking of our church; to us it is so important.'

Charles allowed himself to be drawn into the circle round the table. Vera was there, and Madame Joukovsky, and a man, with a long fair moustache, hiding a weak mouth. He was known to drink heavily, but he had preserved – besides an ephemeral title – a certain polished elegance of manner, which made Madame Leonidov say after each one of his visits, *'Quel grand charmeur que le comte!'* Today, however, she seemed to have forgotten his charm, and talked only to Charles. She told him of the difficulties they had in paying for their church, and repeated what he had often heard from her lips – how very dear it was to them and how closely it drew them together in their exile.

'But, Mr Wilson,' she continued, raising her voice to draw the others' attention to the new and interesting thing she was going to suggest, 'perhaps you would like to come with us on Sunday. It is a great feast and the service will be so beautiful.'

'I should be delighted, Madame, but – ' he knew that he did not want to go; that 'church' where he went in company with Lucy, who on Sundays wore a pair of lemon-coloured gloves, so that the damp greyness of the narrow, pillared building was in his mind always connected with them, bored and irritated him. She did not give him time to make an excuse, but went on to speak about meeting him, about the best time to meet, the frock that Irochka should wear, and the meal which they would have after their church-going. All these thoughts followed one another so quickly that it was too late to protest when she said in a tone of finality, as though she had concluded a long argument, 'Well, then, it is settled. We will join you tomorrow at eleven o'clock.'

As usual the next day was very fine. Charles decided that spring, if one could use of it a word so charged with a sense of vain expectation and delay, was perfect in Malta. In England he had always hated it. It was connected in his mind not only with the memory of wind and cold, but with so much conversation and neighbourly friendliness. Whenever he went out, he heard the same people address the same remarks to each other, as earnestly as if they were convinced that no one had ever said them before. People behaved as if they believed that their fuss about the first flower, and their letters about the first cuckoo, made the spring come more quickly, and that when at last it had struggled into deceptive warmth the greater part of the credit was due to them.

But here it was an imperceptible blossoming out of all that had mysteriously sapped life from wind and rain during the winter months. As Charles stood waiting beneath the plaster figure of a saint in a niche over the door of a shop of curios, he thought with sullen anger of the English spring, the cold, the rain, the stupid faded daffodils and primroses which women and children held out at every street corner. Madame Leonidov was never punctual and he had a third time refused the *carrozin*, whose driver had three times stopped in front of him, when at last she appeared. He at once realised that he had been kept waiting because she had spent more time than usual on her appearance. She certainly looked magnificent.

The gleaming light, which was especially noticeable about her in strong sunshine, formed an aureole round her head, and divided into countless flashes in the folds of her black silk dress. She walked with such implacable stateliness that no beggar dared stop her on her way. She was one of the few whose progress through the streets of the town was never impeded. There was a look of concentration on her face, as if she were about to perform a grave duty, to which she alone with her majesty and composure was truly equal. Charles joined the short procession which followed her: Irochka in very frilled skirts and a large hat which flapped as she walked; Maria Ivanovna, and Abramovitch, wearing a stiff high collar, in which his thin neck moved uneasily as though seeking to escape from imprisonment. They walked in silence till they reached the quay and crossed to Sliema in a *dghaisa*, which Madame Leonidov carefully chose because 'the man looks more safe. I always fear accidents.'

For the same reason she never took a *carrozin*, being certain that a wheel might at any moment come off its axle and precipitate her on the ground.

Their way through the streets of Sliema was accompanied by the clamour of church bells. At every corner they were greeted by another peal, till Charles longed for escape from the clanging noise. At last they reached a large, grey house, distinguished from others by a very small, gilt cross, which lurked on the roof among several chimneys. For the last time Madame Leonidov turned to rally them round her and went in. Charles wanted to laugh. He gave Maria Ivanovna a self-conscious smile and murmured, 'I feel terribly nervous,' but she did not answer. Leaving the sound of bells behind them, they passed into a narrow passage, through folding doors which swung silently on their hinges. Charles felt rather than saw that everything was covered with red baize, and that men talking in whispers stood along the walls.

Several of them kissed Madame Leonidov's hand as she passed. He could see the black plume of her hat, nodding from side to side. At last the passage widened into a room, and Charles found himself standing on red baize behind a woman who knelt in front of a chair. The crowd at the entrance had separated him from Madame Leonidov, whom he saw buying a candle at a table on the right. He watched her push Irochka up to the gilded barrier raised by two steps from the floor, and stop to talk to some friends, while the girl stuck her candle on a candlestick, where many others already burned. The choir, whom Charles could not see, although he craned his neck in all directions, were singing a rhythmical melody which pleased him. He was sorry when they stopped abruptly, and a priest came out of a side door. He turned to face the golden barrier and began to intone in a deep bass, bowing every time he allowed his voice to drop after a long note.

The people followed him, making the sign of the cross, and even kneeling to get up again very quickly. Charles noticed that everyone did what he liked. The woman in front of him had remained on her knees since the beginning of the service; out of the corner of his eye he could see two men talking together. Close by, a young woman, with very fair hair under a black hat with a drooping brim, was trying to soothe a little girl. She had placed her gloves on a chair in front of her and one of them kept falling off. She would stoop to pick it up and replace it on the edge so that it fell off again.

'What with the child and the gloves,' thought Charles, 'she hasn't got much time to say her prayers.' The priest, whose voice filled the small room with torrents of sound, was visibly growing exhausted. Charles watched the folds of skin on his short, thick neck redden and the thin hair above his red ears grow damp. The room was suffocatingly hot. Standing with his crushed hat in his hand, when at any moment the kneeling woman in front of him might trip him up with her long skirt, he felt exhausted. His back and feet ached, and he thought it would be a relief to kneel down. The vacillating light of the many guttering candles and the smell of grease and myrrh made him feel dizzy and sick. If only he could sit down on one of those chairs by the walls, but obviously they were only for the use of women, and besides, he was afraid to move lest someone should speak to him. To distract his attention from his aching limbs, he fixed his eyes on Madame Leonidov. She seemed to be more devout than anyone he had so far noticed. Her ungloved right hand moved with the regularity of a pendulum from her forehead to her breast. She knelt frequently; she bowed so low that the plume in her hat swept the ground. He saw her poke Irochka in the small of the back, so that Irochka, who, judging by her yawns and fidgeting hands, was very bored, should kneel down too. Near them was Vera, in the same coat too tight for her under the armpits, praying with a concentration which lent her face, with its hooked nose and full protruding chin, the look of a hungry chicken, forced from lack of food to look up from the unfruitful ground towards the even more unfruitful sky. Clasped in her red hands she held a large black reticule.

'Why on earth doesn't she put it down?' he thought. 'How stupid people look when they are praying. And is she praying?' A vague wonder stirred in him at these people, standing, kneeling, bowing, crowded together in a small stuffy room with its ceiling painted a blue that had faded, but was here and there still bespangled with ten-rayed stars. What power drew them together to pray in front of closed gilded doors with an edge of dark curtain showing above them, and long strips of canvas painted with flat-faced boneless figures of angels and saints? There was one on the right, with a silver halo and red robes. He looked a little like Abramovitch. In his hands he held an object rather like a box.

'Looking at his pebbles,' thought Charles, and immediately saw the emaciated figure of Abramovitch, clad in red robes, his thin long neck moving uneasily in his collar, his greyish beard turned to silver, wandering on the outskirts of heaven in search for precious specimens. Poor Abramovitch, how pitiful he was with all his pessimism and his

81

philosophizing! As he looked at the expressionless faces of the painted saints, he felt pity for the people who stood before them. Lately he had heard much about the Russian's religion, and he had expected to be impressed, but so far there had been nothing to impress him. It seemed rather a haphazard form of worship. A little, he thought, like going to a play knowing exactly when one had to applaud. Except that in theatres one could at least sit, and here this standing business was awful. The service seemed nowhere near an end, and it was quite impossible to get out. Turning his head to see how far he was from the door, he noticed the count who had such a reputation for insobriety and charm, and wondered what satisfaction he could derive from all this dazzling gold, from the candles, guttering on to the dusty red carpet, from the painted saints, who swayed so pathetically every time anyone passed behind them. The deep-voiced priest had at last stopped his recitation. He had pushed open Abramovitch, who apparently served as a door, and had vanished. Somebody pulled at the curtain Charles had noticed behind the golden gates. There was a pause and nearly everyone knelt down. With a feeling of apprehension at the sudden hush which had fallen on the room, he too knelt down.

The choir began to sing and clouds of incense rose from behind the gates towards the blue ceiling. Charles could only see the faces round him through a dusty haze; several women took out their handkerchiefs; he heard a stifled sob and the whine of a child somewhere at the back. The singing had grown very beautiful; it was not like church music as he knew it from regular attendance at Mattins or from the choir practices his father used to hold on Thursday nights in the draughty parish room. There was something wistful about these voices which betrayed no straining after rhythm, but sang in effortless harmony, as though the singers knew that the air they breathed out would, independently of them, transfuse into melody. There might have been words, but Charles was aware only of the melancholy which overwhelmed him with the poignancy of the first sorrows of childhood. It had the soothing power of tears. It was like those dreams from which the sleeper has to wake before he knows that they are sad.

He was so completely mastered by this emotion that no part of his reason seemed free from it to break the spell and reproach him with sentimentality. He was like a prisoner, fettered by his own chains and oblivious of their weight.

He did not see how the golden door opened and how a row of priests appeared, each motionless, each holding something. They stood upright, almost as though on tiptoe, like the carved figures with their stone feet pointing downwards round the doors of a Gothic cathedral. The people bowed; Charles bowed with them. When he straightened his back he saw Maria Ivanovna, of whom he had not thought since he had entered the church, and who at once seemed the only person in it. Her face was raised as if towards the ray of sunshine which pierced one of the narrow windows and hung in the dusty air. Although very still, she did not seem absorbed in prayer; on the contrary, it struck Charles that she had not shared in the common emotion, but that the whole of her being was concentrated on one thought, one vital impulse complete in itself. She was kneeling in front of a low altar, on which lay a large icon, surrounded by a fading wreath of white flowers. Charles was so near that he could see the face framed in its embossed silver nimbus. It was the face of a Madonna, like any face on any icon, faded, dark, but not featureless. In its narrow oval was concentrated a world of grief; the head bowed on the thin neck in sadness, the eyebrows – a thin dark curve – were raised as though in astonishment. The candles, burning before the altar, let fall upon it the mellow warmth of their light, which mingled with the luminous ray, poised like a dart in flight too swift to be reckoned, above Maria Ivanovna's head. Charles looked at her face and saw in it the reflection of the questioning sorrow which lingered over the dark features of the Madonna. In a flash of blinding insight, it revealed to him his love for her. He knew at last that freedom and happiness were hidden from him no longer because he could find them in her.

It was like the simple, obvious solution of a child's puzzle. He felt no surprise and no misgivings; everything outside his emotion ceased to matter. He forgot where he was; out of a darkness studded with innumerable points of light which flickered like candle flames he wanted to reach her, he wanted to call out to her and make her hear him. But the words he was unconsciously muttering caused someone to turn round, with a glance which conveyed very clearly to his reason that he was being a nuisance. Afraid of looking up, he knelt on the carpet with the smell of dirty stuff and candle grease in his nostrils, but although he did not again raise his head, her image was so clear in his mind that his eyes could not have added another detail to it. He closed them against the light and the dark shapes which had begun to move round him. It was not until he felt a stream of fresh air down his back that he realised that he wanted to go out. He rose from his knees with cramped, aching joints. The doors had been opened. A great many people had already left, but there were still chattering groups of them at the back, and a small crowd round a priest, who stood on the steps, holding out a cross. Men in black roamed about, putting out candles and removing chairs. An atmosphere of discreet hurry had taken the place of solemnity. Charles picked up his battered hat and went out. At the door an old man holding a bronze plate stopped him. He wore a grey overcoat of military cut with a great many collars, revers and red tabs. A star dangled from his neck on a frayed black ribbon. His face had the look of ingrained unhappiness, which is most often seen in those who in their struggle against implacable adversity have completely lost the power of mirth. He muttered something between toothless gums.

'What does he want of me?' thought Charles; 'he has five wrinkles on his forehead and he looks dirty.' But he gave him nothing. In the street he did not see Madame Leonidov and the others. Probably they had forgotten about him.

Instead of going to the Villa, where he was expected to lunch, he wandered aimlessly about the streets, empty now because from every kitchen came the greasy smell of the midday meal which had claimed the presence of loiterers. Once Charles stopped for a drink because his throat felt parched, but he did not know where he was. He remembered only that the hand which gave him the glass had dirty nails and thick, black hairs on the finger joints. A feeling of disgust came over him and he pocketed the coin he had placed on the marble slab.

The sensation of great happiness which he had experienced in the church deserted him, to give place to anxiety. The same thoughts whirled in his mind, like the spokes of a revolving wheel, which he had not the power to stop. He must find her, see her as soon as he could; when he saw her he would take her hand and say, 'Maria Ivanovna,' quietly so as not to frighten her, 'Maria Ivanovna.' But first he must find her – find her. At last he stopped in a narrow street, across which garments had been hung on a line to dry. The clear definite shadows of trousers and shirts on the walls of the houses reminded him that it would soon be tea time (habit had made of his meals the landmarks of his day). He looked at his watch. It was past three and he was still in Sliema. He would take over an hour getting up to the Villa, and as if on purpose he could hear nowhere the jingling bells of a *carrozin*. Afraid that after all he would miss Maria Ivanovna – she might go out, perhaps – he ran a good deal of the way, so that he was out of breath when he reached the garden gate. It creaked on its hinges as he opened it. He stopped to fix the latch, remembering Madame Leonidov's words –

'Dear Mr Wilson, if you would be good to take guard that the little gate is always shut. If it is left open the dogs and the children come in . . .' The thought of her restored his self-possession. His hair was probably very untidy. He put on his hat and wiped his hot face. He wandered up the path slowly, kicking at the wooden steps, anxious to retard the moment when he should have to walk into the drawing-room.

Outside the door he met Maria Ivanovna, who came round the corner of the house with a broken doll in her hands. (Madame Leonidov would often say, 'Irochka is so careless. Just like her father, *pauvre enfant*.')

'Oh,' said Charles blankly, and stopped, not knowing what he should do now that chance favoured him so surprisingly. She had stopped too, as though she expected him to say something. At last he managed to stammer:

'It is so fine now; isn't it a pity to go in? Won't you come for a walk?' It seemed to him that hours passed before her voice reached him from somewhere very far away.

'Yes, I should like to. I will just leave this doll. Irochka has been in a bad temper again.' Bless her, she hadn't suggested that he should go in, as he feared she might. Only another moment and she would come out to him.

Her face, her voice, the whole of her wonderful presence would be alone with him, unshared by others.

They walked in silence along the narrow road, which led past the house, into the fields beyond. The sun was hot and there was no wind. A flock of birds crossed the sky in steady flight out towards the sea. Maria Ivanovna watched them until their line had become a faint streak across the horizon. She had pointed them out to Charles, but he had taken no notice of them. He was absorbed in his happiness. He had been afraid of seeing her, as one fears to look again on that which one has greatly admired, lest it should deceive and prove unworthy of admiration, but he had at once regained the confidence with which she always inspired him. He felt that he could continue walking with her for ever, leaving the town and the rest of the world behind, and moving as it seemed to him higher, onward towards a pale sky, veiled in mist beyond the farthest hill that he could see. It was a relief to him that he felt no need to explain himself. He did not want to make love to her, to awaken her to the feelings which stirred within him. He was even strangely impatient of the few remarks which passed between them. She had won him over to her silence and passivity.

They wandered along the bright-coloured enclosures, which owing to the smallness of their expanse could hardly be called fields: now clover, now young wheat in rivalry with the poppy or thick-stalked daisies. Sometimes a tree planted at the corner formed by two stone walls, like a lonely bulwark against wind and rain, broke the monotony of those cultivated squares which in Charles's eyes transformed the landscape into an uneven patchwork, divided only by the twisting, yellow roads. They stopped by a wall which separated them from a vineyard sloping down the side of the hill, because Maria Ivanovna wanted to pick some flowers which grew on the bank. The noise of rattling stones quite close made them pause and listen to the only sound which broke the silence. Suddenly a voice began to sing, startling them because they had thought themselves alone. At first slowly and softly, then louder, with a nasal drawl it sang. 'Ave Maria, A-a-ve Maria,' it repeated with obstinate insistence on every note, as though the singer were afraid to lose one fraction of the sound value, 'A-a-ve Maria-a-a.' The rattling of stones came nearer.

'It's probably somebody pushing a barrow down the hill,' said Charles. 'Let's go on.' They walked on, followed by the voice, which gradually grew fainter. The last 'Ave Maria' reached them like the twang of a guitar quickly silenced by a player, impatient of its sound. They had now come to an open track of country where the grass was long and the flowers rare. Only the pale, fragile campanulas, as though worn out by the sun, bowed their heads beneath their feet. A light wind passed in luminous tracks over the grass. It made long, furrow-like shadows which crept along, thinning as they retreated farther away.

Maria Ivanovna walked quickly towards a rise, which would reveal the sea, now hidden by a bend. The daisies and thistles growing in thick patches on the hillock clung to her feet, and fastened themselves to the hem of her dress. She hurried on till at last she ran up the slope, leaving Charles behind, and when she had reached the top turned towards the sun. The wind caught her dress and made it stream out like a white sail. Her hair was blown from her face. She let her hands drop to her sides and the flowers she had held scattered at her feet. She looked towards the sea, which lay calm and wrapped in a haze such as rises at dawn or precedes the sunset, when the day has been hot and windless. The thin, curling smoke which rose from the boats in the harbour hung like a web above it. It was the same view that they were accustomed to see every day from the Villa, but distance lent it more beauty, just as it lent an added gleam to the white, terraced houses of Valletta.

'Oh, look,' she said, and turned towards him. But his eyes silenced her, and she raised her hand as if to shield herself from danger. He knelt down before her, his face against her breast; then he felt her hands on his hair. They did not speak, but had he looked up he might again have seen in her wistful look the reflection of the puzzled, grieving face of the dark icon framed in white, fading flowers.

The silence, which comes with the evening, had fallen. Even the wind had dropped, as though hiding in the grass. Nothing stirred about them until a bird, scared out of its refuge, rose with a whir of wings from the ground. For a moment it twittered about their heads, then soared into the sky, leaving them once more to the wakeful silence of the earth.

VI

CHARLES DID NOT ATTEMPT to struggle against his feelings for Maria Ivanovna because the ideas of morality, which he had for twenty years of his life applied in his judgement of others, were completely driven out of his mind by his love.

In the first hours which followed their separation from each other he had tried to persuade himself of his folly. Conscientiously, as though he were fulfilling a duty he owed himself, he forced into his mind memories which should have dispelled his illusion, memories of the old vicarage at Elmshurst-on-Trent, with the two stunted yew trees in green tubs on the lawn; the heavy, brown curtains in his father's study (when as a small boy he had stood there, before an irate parent, his eyes had used to travel up and down them, trying to count the flies, which lived in their folds); the colour of Lucy's hair; the smell of the gas stove in the kitchen. Reluctantly those images rose to the surface of his mind and vanished again. Facts no longer mattered to him. He had reached that stage of self-forgetfulness when it is possible to act without first pausing to think of consequences, because the mind has no thought for what will come afterwards. When for a short time the haunting sense of the future vanishes, it is unshackled by fears and prompts actions from which it might otherwise have shrunk. Consequently the scruples which a month ago would have preoccupied Charles did not occur to him now. He was not afraid that by concealing the truth he might wreck his own happiness; in his present state of exaltation that would have seemed impossible. He could have no doubts that it would not be complete and lasting. He was overwhelmed by desire for her; every other feeling in him was deadened by his craving; it swept him into a realm of emotions that he had never known.

She accepted his love without surprise, almost as though she had a right to expect it. Serenely she had yielded to him. Only the strange look which sometimes troubled him had not vanished from her eyes: a look of inconsolable sadness, as if she regretted her surrender to his will.

In the days which followed the beginning of their love Charles made his happiness as safe as he could. He severed all his ties with a past which had assumed in his eyes the worthlessness of an old, worn-out garment. He did not hesitate in doing this. His indecision vanished before the fear of losing Maria Ivanovna. He overcame his scruples at deceiving her by telling himself that later would do. He would reveal his secret when he was quite sure of her – sure that she would forgive him. He wrote to his wife, saying that he had been ordered to join a ship which was to call at Malta on her way to the East, and would consequently not be able to return home. He then completed his renunciation of his old self by informing his Company that he wished to retire immediately on account of ill-health. At least for the present he had sufficient means for himself. His wife could get all she wanted from her mother. He knew the old woman was well off, or she wouldn't have gone on blessing the memory of her late husband twelve years after his death. Charles felt no regret for his wife and his children. He did not love them, because they too closely resembled their mother. Lucy did not care for him; she would console herself easily enough. Their marriage had been a terrible mistake; irksome to her, humiliating to him. Only complete apathy had prevented him from breaking their union. But now at last he had shaken off his indifference. His love for Maria Ivanovna filled him with energy and longing to forget his weaknesses. His life no longer seemed a failure. He thought of it as a long happiness with her, who by some miracle had woken him from his apathy. He found that he had new ideals and that he despised himself for having lived with a woman with whom his only bond was custom. The usual code inflicted on him by his upbringing and his class had lost all its meaning for him. The righteousness he had observed as part of his narrow-minded creed now seemed the greatest of the prejudices with which his life had always been cramped. He was now determined to free himself from them. He wanted to live without restraint, unhampered by the laws and customs which men had made in defiance of nature. He was too absorbed in himself, too full of his grievances and his delight in his new salvation to realise that he was only one of the great many who, having made havoc of their lives, turn to that idealism which they label as

'Nature', and blame mankind and the society in which they move for their failure and their unhappiness. His love only made him pass from one selfishness to another. He never paused to wonder whether Maria Ivanovna would consider him as guiltless as he thought himself. He warded off danger by shutting his eyes to it, and hedged himself in so as to be able to enjoy the happiness which liberal hands were ready to give him.

His love grew with every hour he spent in her presence. The look of peaceful joy which had settled on her face charmed him because it brought the knowledge that it was he who caused it. She accepted his passion with deep contentment, but she still baffled him. He could never feel that he had bound her to himself. She was herself as intangible as her beauty, which was not confined to her face and her body – it was not as it were fixed in them, but seemed to flow into them from a vital source, hidden beneath her tranquillity. Charles, who under the stimulus of her imagination had begun to find the expression of ideas easier and more natural, compared it in his mind to the sea, which when a wind near the shore stirs its surface, reveals beneath its uniform blue another colour, the reflection not of the sky, but, were that possible, of its mysterious, unexplored depths.

These thoughts did not content him entirely; there were moments when he seemed to lose contact with her, when he felt that he was pursuing something illusive, the essence of her spirit, which, try as he would, he was not able to capture. Then he would grow discouraged; reproach her for not understanding him and protest that he was not good enough for her. But her tenderness always restored his calm and he would regain his assurance in her surrender.

One day, however, she dispelled his sense of security. They had gone out along the coast beyond St Julian's Bay, and had spent many hours roaming in the deserted country. They had loitered, not realising how much time had passed, until they found that they had lost their way. They could not retrace their steps to the main road, and in the hope of reaching some village struck out on a dusty track, which led farther inland. At last it brought them to a lonely group of huts sheltering against the slope of a hill. The small, closely shuttered houses looked empty. There was no one about. Only a goat with bright, amber-coloured eyes raised its inquisitive head to look at them, straining at the thin rope to which it was tethered, and a lean dog with a tail too long for its body continued unperturbed to scratch his back against a wall. Charles knocked loudly on a half-open door. A woman, with a blue shawl sliding off her black hair and fastened on her breast with a large gold pin, came out and stared at them. Charles explained that they wanted to know the way, and asked if she could give them something to drink. She pointed to the goat, but when he shook his head she let a flow of words escape her lips. They understood that she had some wine, although of course they would have to pay more.

She then led them into a courtyard with low wooden benches against the walls, and brought a jug of thin reddish liquid, which tasted sour, but not unpleasant. For a while they sat in silence. With his hand on her hot, smooth arm, he watched her, wondering what she could be thinking about. The pensive look in her eyes disconcerted him. She would sometimes gaze at nothing for hours, not heeding him at all. It was hardly day-dreaming, rare in those who are happy and know that they are loved, but a state of quiescence which he could not understand, and which made him feel almost as if he wasn't wanted. She had been like that today; absent-minded – listless.

'Dearest,' he said, 'what are you thinking about? Not of me, I am sure.' 'Yes,' she replied, smiling at him, 'I was thinking of you and wondering what makes you a little like a Russian.'

'A Russian, why?' He spoke uneasily because he still shrank from being associated with Russians and avoided the thought that she was one.

'Because you don't talk about facts and things that happen, but about your thoughts and feelings. Some Russians always do that, like in Chekov's plays, you know.'

'What do you mean?'

'Well, you have told me nothing about yourself and your life before you came to Malta.'

'It only began then,' he replied, but the words sounded forced and exaggerated. He was annoyed. He had not expected an answer which might almost be a challenge. Could her suspicions have been roused? Had anybody been talking to her? There was no one who knew about him except Homoutov, and he was safe in Madagascar. When he came back – well, there was still time. Although her remark must only have been the result of her thoughts, he felt uneasy and tried hard not to show it. The laugh he gave to cover his embarrassment sounded quite unnatural even in his own cars.

'My dear, if you say I am like a Russian, then you are like the English girls, who cannot rest until they have found all about their lover's relations and friends.'

She looked at him seriously, as though trying to arrive at the meaning of his words.

'You accuse me quite wrongly. It is not that at all,' she said, and let the hands he had been holding drop into her lap. Charles was always at a loss how to interpret her silences. Perhaps he had offended her; perhaps he had offended her a hundred times like this, and a hundred times she had hidden it from him. He was a clumsy fool. It seemed to him, as it had often seemed before, that he had never loved her as much as at that moment. He was overwhelmed with tenderness, because her tired face looked beautiful, and because he had to admit that he was betraying her. Only the fear that she would not bear it prevented him from telling her everything now. He dared not risk it. He might kill her love, or if he did not he might make a wound too deep to heal perhaps. She would conceal it from him, suffer alone. He shrank from the thought of hurting her. Better leave well alone, now. Later, when he was more sure of her, when he himself had got accustomed to the idea. He was half-conscious of the fact that by putting off the unpleasant he was indulging the same cowardice which, when he was a child, had made him wait till the last possible moment before confessing that it was he who had stolen the jam.

Maria Ivanovna was speaking again.

'I am not inquisitive,' she said, as if determined to justify herself, 'but the memories of my childhood, of all my past life, are very precious to me. I can't explain why, but I hoped you would feel the same; that I would be able to share in all that you remembered about yourself. But of course, we have so much time for that; when we are married and . . .' His movement of surprise made her break off and look at him.

'What is the matter?' she asked.

'Nothing, only a fly. Beastly things.' He was completely taken aback. He felt as if he had been walking on ground which, before he was aware of it, had become a bog. He cursed himself bitterly for his folly. Marriage! He had thought of it, of course, but in a dim, uncertain future, which would come 'later', not as a fact that one could talk about. He suddenly realised that his love-making must have been unusual, because he had never spoken of this business. She did not seem to want words and promises; he thought that she was content to take him as he was – entirely absorbed in the present. Marry her! Good Lord! – it was one thing to love a woman, and be loved by her, but all his ingrained prejudices, his fear of anything openly immoral, was up in arms against this dreadful idea. He was not going to behave like a blackguard and treat her dishonourably. He repeated the word over and over again. It had something solid and tangible and comforting about it, a word which had a very special meaning in Bayswater and Golders Green.

Fortunately she did not appear to notice his confused silence. At last, when the sunlight in which they had sat receded into a thin wedge above Maria Ivanovna's head, and the rest of the courtyard was in shadow, Charles said. 'Let's go home. It will take us some time to get back.'

The woman in the blue shawl was still standing in the doorway. As he dropped a coin into her dirty hand Charles looked into her face. Her narrow, black eyes were very sly. She shook her head, and, coming up closer to him, hissed something into his ear, and he felt her breath hot and smelling of garlic on his face. Then she burst into silent laughter, which shook her body as a lean hack is shaken by a cough. He pushed past her and went out into the road. There was something uncanny about the whole place; those forsaken hovels and this woman alone with her blue shawl and foul words, ugh! He hurried Maria Ivanovna away.

It was late when they reached the Villa. Madame Leonidov greeted them coldly with questions as to what could have kept them so long. This was not the first time she had treated them with studied indifference, as if she were a little bored by their society and did not mind showing it. He could not make up his mind as to what provoked this cold, mocking anger to which she gave vent through stinging allusions and remarks disguised like needles in a bolster by her soft, beautiful voice. At supper – Vera Bernini was there, of course – she talked about the freedom of this post-war time, of the great changes it had wrought in what she always referred to as the *mœurs* of life; and thanked God that she had no grown-up daughters. When Irochka giggled at this she rebuked her with a sharpness which silenced not only the offender but also everyone else. Afterwards, instead of sitting down to play patience, she swept from the room, leaving behind her a feeling of uneasiness and constraint which settled on them like a thin, clammy mist, which does not lift until wind and rain sweep it away. Charles had hoped in vain that Vera would go too, because she had taken to following Madame Leonidov about, with an expression of humility and devotion which seemed alien to the slightly arrogant expression on her face, and which she seemed to keep there by a great effort of will. She would often look up at her benefactress, as she had now begun to call her, with glistening eyes, and now and then press her hand between her thick red fingers. All this served to convince Charles that she was hypocritical, jealous and pushing. She had stopped making herself agreeable to him, but he felt that he was being watched by her.

He frequently came across her in the passages, in the garden, in the streets even, whereas before he had rarely met her except in the drawing-room of the Villa.

Directly after supper she had taken up her position on the sofa, entrenched behind the shadow of the lamp, and she sat there, a thin, acid smile on her lips, her eyes darting about the room. She made several remarks to Abramovitch, who was more glum than ever and hardly answered her. Charles tried to talk to Maria Ivanovna, but in front of these people there was nothing to talk about. Besides, he was still tingling with resentment at this afternoon's incident. Wasn't she showing indecent eagerness to get him as quickly as she could? Perhaps it was all an intrigue between these wretched foreigners. Cynically, and at heart pleased with his cynicism, which made him feel that he was being cleverer and more astute than all these people round him, he assured himself that it was of course their doing. They had wanted to bring him and Maria Ivanovna together so as to get rid of her (he realised now that not even Madame Leonidov, despite her show of affection, cared for her), and now they were beginning to be afraid that nothing would come of their well-laid plans. What could they be after? Surely not money? They must know that he hadn't much, and besides Madame Leonidov had plenty of her own, although she always complained bitterly of her poverty. Homoutov himself had told her that she was mean, and Maria Ivanovna had been a burden on her. Why had he never thought of all this before? He was being gulled by foreigners, who pretended to be so kind-hearted, but were usually on the look-out for what they could get from other people. He was a damned fool for not having seen through Madame Leonidov's insinuations and Vera's spite long ago. It was always like this. He allowed himself to be put upon.

'Yes, Charles, what did I tell you? Serves you right for lending that man ten bob when I warned you he was a thief.' A face and a voice leapt into his mind as though they had jumped out of a box, whose lid had suddenly sprung open. He drove them back, but thoughts, such as he had not had for many weeks, commonplace and dull, followed them in a weary sequence.

What was he doing here getting into embarrassing situations? He imagined he was in love. Much good was it doing him! What would Lucy say if she knew that he was mixing himself up with a woman? Sentimental ass. Foreigners, too; not a single person who wasn't a bit cranky among the lot. Maria Ivanovna? Well, she was strange; he couldn't understand her. Better, perhaps, to leave things as they were and go away before anything happened.

The daring thought made him gasp. He pretended to clear his throat. As though she had been expecting some such signal, Vera turned to him. She adopted the playful tone which irritated Charles even more than her sarcasm. It sounded so affected in French.

'You do not converse much with Maria Ivanovna. You are silent like this always?' Charles glared because he knew that she couldn't see his face. Why should he bother to answer such stupid unnecessary remarks? Fortunately Maria Ivanovna interrupted a silence in which Vera's eyes had grown eloquent with inquisitiveness.

'Why do you want us to talk, Vera? Besides, we might disturb Elena Michailovna with our voices. You know the walls are very thin.'

'Yes, it is impossible to build well in Malta. If there were an earthquake, nothing would remain standing in Sliema and Valletta except the forts.'

'*Quelle bêtise*,' exclaimed Vera resentfully, as if the suggestion of earthquakes in Malta were a personal insult to her. Abramovitch made his usual deprecating gesture, which Charles always thought made him look very Jewish. 'Well, there is much that is perplexing about the structure of the earth,' he said.

('What a waste of time all this is! So like them,' thought Charles.)

'You are always so confident. You never see a hole until you fall into it. There are volcanoes and earthquakes in the islands of Sicily and there is Mount Vesuvius, but people walk about there just as you and I walk here in Malta. They are ignorant and they will not believe that there is danger, even when their houses begin to shake. Life is all like this, is it not?'

Charles looked at him, wondering whether he was in earnest. He sat staring at the floor, his fingers playing with his beard, which always gave Charles the impression that it grew a little to one side of his chin. The light shining in a round patch on his head lent it a reddish glow. The deep folds of skin about his mouth made his face look old, particularly so tonight, when there seemed something dejected and pitiable in his posture.

'What a wreck the man is,' thought Charles, and remembered the night they had wandered about the streets together and Abramovitch, flapping his long arms like a bird with tired wings, had talked and talked. His uneasiness grew under the fire of Vera's glances. He got up. 'Vera Antonovna, if you will excuse me, I will go and smoke outside. It's rather warm in here.'

'The windows are open,' she replied, but he took no notice, and went out without looking at Maria Ivanovna, although he felt her eyes fixed on him.

Outside the air was heavy and damp. The pungent smell of the tobacco plants which grew in untidy clumps round the house rose to his nostrils with excessive sweetness. Their flat, white heads had been battered by yesterday's wind, and in the dark looked like so many scraps of paper on the ground. A bat cut through the air with noiseless wings.

Here there was no relief from the stuffy atmosphere of

the drawing-room. Tonight the sea seemed so far away that not the faintest breath of freshness rose to him from it. He saw, or rather felt, it as a smooth expanse of darkness, beyond the lights of the harbour, merging into a darker sky, and weary of the scented, unnerving stillness about him, he longed for wind or the taste of salt foam on his lips.

He did not want to go back into the house; everything there oppressed him. He felt an absurd longing to go and wake them up by telling them what he thought of them all: Vera, Abramovitch, Madame Leonidov. They lived in this house as in a box, which was never opened, and had the musty smell of old wood.

The thought of that faint, familiar odour of decay nearly made him sneeze. Well, he would go now and not return. If they heard the click of the gate as he opened it, it would be too late to call him back; besides, they would not want him. He somehow could not think of Maria Ivanovna apart from the others. His love seemed to have shrunk like a child's balloon which baffles the efforts of 'grown-ups' by deflating as soon as they have blown it out. There was no room in his heart for emotion; only for an uneasiness which had settled there, and which he could not drive away. It made him feel ridiculous in his own eyes. What a fool he was to play the hero, the lover; to imagine that there was that power in him which could set him above the circumstances of his life! Some lurking sense of right had suddenly woken him from his delusions. Lucy – so sharp-tongued and ready to talk about the obvious – was perhaps not far wrong when she accused him of being a coward. He could not bring himself to face a risk. Unknowingly Maria Ivanovna had brought him to his senses. It was safer to go back, safer to forget that he had loved her and indulged his longing for the unknown and unexplored in his own self. After all, he had only to congratulate himself that he could get off so easily. Not even she knew where he lived in Valletta. He would be able to leave Malta before they had found him. As for her, she would forget him. He had been told often enough that women never cared for a man, only for what he gave them. She was young; she would find another lover.

He had no hat; he could leave his stick. When they heard the gate shut (sounds carried far on such a night) it would be too late to make him return. He started to walk down the path, sideways, as if thus his feet could make less noise. He felt that he must at all cost keep the thought of Maria Ivanovna out of his mind, because a vision of her face, as clear as that of Lucy's had been an hour ago, would break his resolve to go away. Fortunately he was bad at remembering faces. Even the features that were most familiar and dear to him were always playing at hide and seek with his memory. At best he retained a vague impression which in time grew dim and blurred and then vanished altogether.

Of course it was in a way a relief (he swore as he tripped on a loose stone) that he had to force himself to go, that he needed all his courage to extricate himself from a position which would daily grow more uncomfortable. He would pay for his rashness. He would suffer. Was he not haunted by bad luck and doomed to unhappiness?

There was something white near the gate, by that hedge. A blur which might be a human form or a white acacia in flower. Curse his short-sightedness! He was almost blind in the dark. He felt in his pockets for his spectacles, and pulled himself up with a muttered ejaculation as he realised that they would be of no use whatever. He did not take his eyes off the shape, which moved and swayed. He was very near now, but he still could not see. The gate creaked on its hinges. He was a few yards away from it and face to face with Maria Ivanovna. She had turned at the sound of his footsteps.

'What are you doing here?' he said in a voice which expressed no surprise. Again his bad luck!

'Waiting for you. I knew you would not come back into the house.'

'What do you want? Haven't we been together enough today?' What a strange question from a lover! How strange it must sound to her!

'Yes,' she assented, as if the question had not astonished her. 'Forgive me. I could not let you go away, Charles.' He guessed from her voice that she was looking appealingly at him. What did she mean by 'go away'? Surely she could not have guessed what was in his mind? He put an arm round her and tried to make his voice sound calm and protecting.

'You are nervous, my dear. No, I wasn't coming back. I could not stand Vera; besides, what would have been the good? I can't kiss you there.'

He was a bad liar; he could never think of excuses. He knew that he hadn't wanted to kiss her; he wasn't sure that he wanted to now, although he held her in his arms, her head heavy on his breast. Again he felt the temptation to tell her everything. Perhaps it was after all the easiest way.

He was almost certain now that she would not forgive him, wouldn't even attempt to understand. He would be able to leave her with an easy conscience. It was better than divorce, better than marriage with her and a life among foreigners.

Absentmindedly stroking her hair, he wondered how she would take it. Stiffen in his arms and go away with the listless, dragging walk he had noticed when she was tired. She moved then as though in her sleep, so nerveless and mechanical was her step, so impassive her face. He stood looking down at her, trying to find words instead of the emotion which would not stir in his confused, resentful heart.

The silence around them was suddenly interrupted by the sound of footsteps on the other side of the wall.

'Who can it be at this hour?' murmured Charles. A man's head appeared over the gate. He opened it and stumbled over the step. Although it was so dark, Charles recognised him. It was Sorokin, a medical student who sometimes came to the Villa, and talked about medicine in a loud, nervous voice. People said he was clever and had ideas, but he was too impatient, always too much in a hurry. He would appear unexpectedly and stand in the drawing-room (he could never be persuaded to sit down), forcing everyone to listen to his medical talk. He never stayed to a meal, but disappeared as suddenly as he came. No one ever spoke of him when he was not there. Madame Leonidov disliked him, because she said he was vulgar. She had a habit of passing judgements on her guests as soon as they had left. They never varied, so that those who had learnt to expect them would have been surprised if she had not capped Madame Joukovsky's departure with 'She has the brain of a hen, that poor woman,' or the bibulous count's with '*Quel charmeur que le comte!*'

Charles had not seen Sorokin more than twice, but he remembered the man's face with its prominent staring eyes and full sensual lips.

'Sorokin, is that you?' he asked, stepping on to the path. The man raised his head.

'Ah, Mr Wilson, good evening. They are at home? I must go up.' He was out of breath, as if he had been running.

'Why, what's the matter?' said Charles, puzzled that he should be in such a hurry.

'I have come for Abramovitch. Madame Kondratieff is ill. I am afraid she is dying. I want help. Her husband is an idiot.'

Recollecting that Sorokin lived in the same house as the Kondratieffs, that consequently he would be the first person to be called upon to help, he asked if he could do anything.

'No,' answered Sorokin curtly, and lurched forward. A moment later the banging of the front door echoed through the garden. Charles wished he had not questioned the man. Death for him was associated with the thought of the purple veins stretched like swollen cords on his father's neck when he lay struggling for his last breath. It had been awful. He had died slowly, and Charles had expected those veins, like the thin bruises from a whip, to burst before his heart stopped beating. This memory, which he had not been able to forget, seared his mind every time that the thought of death was thrust on him. He himself ignored it. It was best not to think about such things.

'Poor Madame Kondratieff,' murmured Maria Ivanovna; 'she has been ill so long. I don't know what will happen to their child.'

'Where are you going?' said Charles, because she had started to walk up the path.

'Anywhere; back to the house. Anywhere.' Her voice startled him. He could not let her go like this. He would reassure her, comfort her. Something within him cried out that if he did not stop her now, it would be too late afterwards. Death, in the shape of that sinister, hurrying figure which passed a moment ago, would come between them. He felt poignant fear and a longing for her who again seemed precious and wonderful.

'Come back,' he whispered, unable to speak out loud; 'you must not go away now. I want you.'

She turned round, and he led her into that part of the garden which was more neglected than the rest. A dwarf cherry tree grew there and the ground was strewn with the petals of its flowers. The earth released the fragrance it had gathered during the long hours of sunlight. The faint perfume of unseen flowers mingled with the smell of grass trodden down under their feet. A large, flat, white stone, lying there no one knew why, alone gleamed in the darkness, like the pale reflection of an invisible moon.

Unheeded, forgotten, they could stand there all night until the grey dawn should appear between the slender branches of the tree. Not even the crickets disturbed their silence. He held her in his arms, and she let his lips rest on hers, but he knew that her eyes had that look, wistful and mysterious, which even love could not banish from them. No shadow of happiness crept into those dark, unflinching pupils. With his kisses he shut her eyelids and smoothed the line which was like a thin thread across her brow, but it was long before she clung to him and he ceased to feel her heart beat like a captive bird in her throat.

They strove to recapture the joy which a while ago had seemed theirs for ever, but there was only bitterness in their hearts and despair born of anticipated grief. To neither did love bring respite from unsatisfied longing.

The next morning they heard that Madame Kondratieff was dead. Abramovitch had come too late to save her. Madame Leonidov at once made it known that she intended to bear the cost of the funeral and invited everyone, including Charles, to attend it.

VII

NOT LONG AFTER Madame Kondratieff's death Charles
was married to Maria Ivanovna in the Russian church at
Sliema. Madame Leonidov had taken it on herself to see the
matter through, and Charles found himself driven into an
action which he had been determined to avoid. After his
chance meeting with Maria Ivanovna, on the night when he
tried to escape, his resolution to do so was weakened by a
sense that he was struggling against hostile forces. Everything seemed to have conspired against him. The commo-
tion with which Madame Kondratieff's funeral was
attended, owing to the efforts of friends anxious to show
their generosity, had kept her from him except in rare
moments when, hungry for her love, he could not bring
himself to reveal his secret. The fear of losing her tortured
him, even more than the talk he was obliged to hear about
his own marriage. Madame Leonidov never ceased telling
him how happy he made her, who had Maria's future so
much at heart. It would be a joy to have them near her and
watch over them like an affectionate mother. This solicitude embarrassed him more than her coldness. He felt help-

less and imprisoned by the sympathy and kindness that she lavished on him. Besides, he knew that all their friends were aware of his relationship with Maria Ivanovna, and the thought that his love had been made public unnerved him. He could feel confident only when he was unknown and unobserved; but now his self-possession was undermined by the attention which was paid him on all sides. He had an ingrained, traditional fear of scandal. By undeceiving Maria Ivanovna he would become an impostor in the eyes of all the people whose duty it was to expose the culpability of others. He imagined himself the helpless prey of their scorn, unable to escape their mockery and malignant curiosity, more galling to him than censure or neglect. Every word of congratulation he heard seemed to him another blow from an adverse fate. Retreat and escape daily became more impossible.

Meanwhile his fear estranged him from Maria Ivanovna. Her beauty and the happiness it betrayed goaded him into extreme resentment. He could not watch her without bitterness in the days which preceded their marriage. She was wonderful. Even those who only knew her as the 'governess at Madame Leonidov's' became aware of the rare charm which seemed to radiate from her person. Tortured by anxiety and a feeling akin to remorse, Charles grudged her this beauty, this loveliness which he had called forth, but which he could not enjoy. He even wished that he had the courage to destroy it, to shatter her illusion and force her to share his suffering. But he dared not: he could not forget that he loved her, and he was ready to face the risk of ignominy and shame to preserve her happiness to the last possible moment. His weakness and his cowardice could not make him cruel.

Besides, he found excuse in the argument that divorce would be an easy matter. It was a tempting relief to persuade himself that by marrying her he would not lose her. She would be safe in his power, bound to him by a bond which he knew she would not easily break. She was religious; she might not allow him to divorce his wife in order to marry her, and she would then go out of his life as suddenly as she had come into it. He was deceiving her now, but only to make her happy afterwards. He was sure of her love for him, and he, despite his vacillation and cowardice, wanted her, longed for her as a drowning man longs for the rock which will protect him from the waves. To him she still seemed, as in the first days of their love, the safe, undefeated thing to which he could anchor the troubles and failures which formed the record of his life.

So, inspired by the hope that everything would still turn out all right, he gave his silent consent to the marriage, and the ceremony was performed by a priest who spoke with a stutter and fidgeted because his long greyish hair tickled the back of his neck.

Afterwards they returned to the Villa in the *carrozins* which rattled and bumped along the streets, unwillingly dragged by the horses which, decorated with tassels and bells, took no notice of the cracking whips and frequent ejaculations of the coachman, but ambled in spiritless fashion along the road.

Madame Leonidov had insisted on inviting guests to drink the thin, sour champagne and eat the food Maria

Ivanovna had prepared that same morning. She had said that of course they would ask only a few intimate friends, but either the intimate were many or she attached a special meaning to the word, for the drawing-room was crowded with people Charles had never seen. They elbowed each other contentedly in the space free from tables and chairs, forgetful of the occasion which brought them there. In fact, after the first few minutes no one took any notice of Charles and Maria Ivanovna. Even Abramovitch, in a long frock coat which fitted badly over his high shoulders, vanished from Madame Leonidov's side, where he had stood to welcome the guests like a reluctant soldier forced into the front rank by the flight of his comrades. Charles retired into a corner of the room, where he could observe without being noticed, and was just about to thank Providence because there were no English people present, when he heard an English voice. A tall young man dressed in the uniform of the Royal Marines was talking to Vera. Charles moved along the wall till he was within earshot of them.

'You say he is English?' The officer spoke in the flat, monotonous voice Charles knew to be the hallmark of good breeding.

'Yes, his name is Wilson. He lives in London, I think.'

'Doubtless.' The young man laughed a quiet, sarcastic laugh, for as far as Charles could see no reason whatever. Those superior good-looking youths were the most awful asses!

'I used to know a Wilson in the Merchant Service some years ago,' the deliberate voice went on, 'but he was married, I believe. It can't be the same man.'

'Ah, *mais non!*' Vera's shrill giggle reached him as he slipped behind the broad scarlet back of a Dowager Countess from Moscow. He must avoid that Englishman; he hadn't recognised the face, but he had such a rotten memory! It might be someone he knew. Unnoticed, he slipped out of the room and went into the garden. It was deserted, and for a while he walked about and tried to cool his face. What a relief that no one had thought of introducing him to that Englishman. He had thought himself safe from old acquaintances, but he saw now that he would have to be careful. His position was difficult enough without chance meetings like that.

When, a little later, he heard Maria Ivanovna's voice calling him, he had regained his composure and turned to her with a smiling face. She had seen him go and had followed as soon as she could. She looked tired.

'Do you know who that Englishman is?' he asked her.

'No. Elena Michailovna knows him – but she knows everybody.'

'Yes, I wish she didn't. Are these people going to be here all night? '

'I expect they will go soon; but it doesn't matter; we needn't go back there.' She smiled and slipped her hand through his arm. He kissed her, wondering who that officer was and what Vera could have told him. She knew as little about him as they all did, but she could invent; and besides, she had such a love of intrigue that she would willingly have wrenched a secret out of the hearts of the dead.

Rapidly now spring was turning into summer, and the last

traces of the beauty which had come with it were being burnt out by the sun. The hot stones of the streets glared in the light and the winds which swept the island brought no coolness. Even the goats, driven from door to door to the mournful cry of 'Hali-ib, Hali-ib,' had a languid look; and the mules, as if resenting the weight of their baskets, stood wearily bending their heads to the ground. No clouds crossed the sky except towards evening, when a wind passing high above the earth scattered them in flaming tongues over the sunset.

Charles and Maria Ivanovna had moved to Sliema and rarely went to the Villa, because Vera lived there now, and Charles refused to meet her more than was necessary. Besides, it was rumoured that Madame Leonidov was ill. She never left her room and insisted that Abramovitch should be always with her. People said that not even his devotion could stand her nerves and that bitter accusations were daily bandied between the invalid and the doctor. Charles told himself that they were well out of such rows and avoided the society of Russians. It was not difficult. To Maria Ivanovna's reputation of being strange was soon coupled the opinion that her husband was surly and disagreeable. They were not interesting and they were left to themselves. Those who considered themselves endowed with a prophetic insight hinted that the marriage would not turn out as well as one might have supposed. Zvonkoff, who had such a gift for saying amusing things, had remarked that the Englishman *avait l'air un peu louche,* and, he added significantly, 'one never knows.' This verdict was accepted as final, and observers allowed their curiosity to

flag, keeping in mind, lest there should be further developments, that of course as Zvonkoff had said 'one never knew.'

Meanwhile Charles wrestled with disappointment. He
hoped so fervently for happiness with Maria Ivanovna that
his marriage had seemed to him as a conjuring trick which,
as soon as it had been performed, would dispel his cares and
serve as a soporific to his timorous scruples. He had never
dreamt that his supreme remedy could fail, but now he was
obliged to realise its failure. Happiness, which he interpreted as freedom from anxiety, was further from him than
it had ever been before. Not endowed with a great faculty for
passionate emotion, he found only transitory satisfaction in
his love. It did not bring him oblivion; it could not break the
barrier between himself and the woman he loved. The
knowledge that she was too good for him had set up a wall
between them. He was convinced now of what he had
vaguely feared before, that in order to keep her love he
would have to live a lie with her, as he had lived a lie with
Lucy.

With Lucy he had hidden his aspirations; he had striven
to bring himself down to the level of common-sense which
she demanded of him. With Maria Ivanovna he was faced
with the task of deceiving her until chance should frustrate
his purpose. He had been prevented from disclosing his
secret before by the fear that she would spurn him and his
love. Now to that fear was added the sense of her integrity
which would not forgive his weakness. He knew her to be
incapable of mean thoughts and actions, of low ungovernable desires, of anything which deviated from the course of
virtue to her so clear and natural. She would not understand

him. Virtue, even if it was unconscious (she never acted on principle, but from instinctive unlimited goodness), was intolerant. She would be too much overwhelmed by his culpability to pity him, and in pitying keep her love. He felt that he could not but destroy it.

The summer wore on and the time dragged unbearably for Charles. Day after day passed, spent in brooding over the same thing. He grew despondent and irritable. Maria Ivanovna seemed to retreat farther from him. The 'later' he had eagerly expected as a future of happiness had grown into a 'too late' – too late to do anything but wait for the moment when an unknown and dreaded power would levy a final blow at his head and shatter the falsehood which he had built round his life. Malta seemed to him a prison where he was cut off from all escape, tied to a woman whom he loved but who was like a living proof of his guilt.

Often these thoughts would drive him out of the house to wander for hours about the streets. He would walk in the heat oblivious of everything, until the fear that he might be recognised seized him and forced him to hurry back, looking round to see that he was not being followed, keeping in the shadow of the houses, starting when he heard an English voice. Gradually he became obsessed by it. He fell into the habit of avoiding the main streets, and of looking cautiously into a shop before he went in.

Once, when he was on his way home in the early afternoon, when the streets were almost deserted except for some vendor of holy images, undaunted by the heat, Charles was startled to see a man raise his hat to him on the other side of the street. He took no notice; but to his consternation the man, who was accompanied by a small boy, crossed over, apparently determined to speak to him. When Charles saw the face under the shabby black bowler he recognised Kondratieff, the husband of her who had received a place in Madame Leonidov's memory as *'cette pauvre Sophie'*. He seemed to have aged since the day of the funeral, when Charles had first seen him. Buttoned into a long coat of black alpaca, with his bowler and short, square beard, he looked like a retired waiter. His son had a large head on a thin neck and very bright pink cheeks, which contrasted painfully with his ill-formed body.

'Consumption,' thought Charles, and wondered what they could want with him. Kondratieff asked after Maria Ivanovna and thanked him for some little objects (Charles could not gather what they were from his halting English) she had sent his son. He was very grateful. It was very kind to remember them.

'Oh, that's all right,' said Charles, anxious to interrupt the mumbling voice. 'And how are you?' He had thought this a safe question; but the man's large, watery eyes filled with tears and he made a gesture which only increased his resemblance to an apologetic waiter listening to the complaints of his customers.

'My poor wife,' he said. 'Madame Leonidov was very kind, but . . .'

'Yes, I am sure.' Charles was relieved to see the little boy tug at his father's sleeve as if he too realised that the situation was growing awkward.

'You must come and see us,' he added, feeling that he must make some effort to show his sympathy. 'Maria

Ivanovna (he never spoke of her as "my wife") would be delighted.'

He went away without stopping to wait for the end of Kondratieff's grateful mumbling. It all seemed so excessive to him. These Russians had no self-control. He shook himself free from the thought of the man's eyes, moist and humble like a dog's.

That meeting was not the last. As though they had been shadows left behind by mistake of that Madame Kondratieff, whose untimely death he sometimes blamed for his unhappiness, he often met the two mournful figures walking slowly hand in hand; and when they drew level with him on the other side of the street Kondratieff would slowly raise his bowler and pass without turning his head, urged forward by the little boy, who pulled at his sleeve.

Charles's fears made him suspicious of every circumstance which seemed to him significant and unprecedented. He began to watch Maria Ivanovna, putting his own interpretation on the least thing she did. Sometimes he imagined that her most ordinary remarks had a double meaning, and he would torture her with questions. It was a relief to give way to words which an outsider would have thought were caused by jealousy. He made her repeat again and again that she loved him and that whatever happened she would never leave him. Thus he cheated himself, and in her arms – her lips on his, the sound of her voice a little weary in his ears – he would forget himself and go back in his mind to the ecstasy of their first hours together. But even in these stolen moments of happiness that memory was tormenting and bitter.

In July Charles was once again forced to take an unwilling part in the life of Russian society.

It was decided that to mend their fortunes, at least temporarily, they would arrange a bazaar to take place in the hall and gardens of an hotel in Sliema. No one quite knew where the idea had originated; probably in the fertile brain of Zvonkoff, who had been at such a function in London, where the committee had done very well out of the profits. Madame Leonidov sacrificed her health on the altar of unselfishness in order to place herself at the head of a group of people ready to devote themselves to the common cause.

'As a capable woman,' she had said, 'I take precedence over the Countess.' And no one had contradicted her. She never allowed it to be forgotten that she alone was fitted to bear the burden of leadership. She declared that the main object of the bazaar was to attract the English and consequently many entertainments were planned.

Madame Vasht, on a short holiday in Malta before a tour over the less populated parts of the world, promised to dance. Madame Nikitin, the florid widow of an undistinguished officer, was anxious to sing. Women who for months had lived inconspicuous and forgotten came forward eager to demonstrate their talents and to receive a fitting reward for their labours. It required all the ingenuity of Madame Leonidov to obtain her own ends without causing severe division among her helpers. As it was, the whole bazaar was nearly wrecked in the dispute which arose between the obstinate creatrix of paper pictures and the no less obstinate Vera, whose originality and taste were to be represented at the needlework stall. Madame Leonidov's patience was taxed beyond endurance. She resigned from the committee, and the doors of the Villa were closed to all comers until she was appeased by a deputation of the most prominent members of Russian society headed by General Koubakin, whose unquestioned authority rested on a beard *à la* Tolstoy and a stentorian voice which held everyone at a distance – a fact attributed by him to his dignity.

Charles watched these developments with profound boredom. Maria Ivanovna was forced to spend all her time at the Villa and Charles became an unwilling witness of the preparations, which dragged on for several weeks. If he did not come Madame Leonidov never failed to remark:

'And where is Charles? Does he not want to help us?'

So he sat for hours in a drawing-room littered with papers and covered in dust. People he did not know walked about the house talking in loud, hurried voices. The front door banged incessantly. Madame Leonidov protested that she had not slept for weeks, and Irochka, left to devour the sweets made in the kitchen, suffered from continuous attacks of indigestion.

The only person who seemed unaffected by this disturbance was Abramovitch. He had been banished to live in Valetta, because Madame Leonidov wanted more room in the house, and he was delighted with his new liberty. He was willing to joke with Charles about the women's 'fussy ways', and even told him that he was about to make an important geological discovery which would add much to that science. Charles expressed his surprise that he did not study medicine.

'Oh,' he replied with a shrug, 'I have given it up long ago. As a doctor I am no good now, except to give Irochka castor oil.'

Secretly Charles wondered at the man's devotion to Madame Leonidov. She was still beautiful; she still retained the power to fascinate; but she was tyrannical, and he had lately learned that she was hard-hearted. She concealed the lack of emotion within her by displaying its outward signs with a regularity which was sufficient to betray her. She wept because tears made her eyes shine and lent her face an expression which she could not achieve without their aid.

The day which Charles dreaded came at last, preceded by a thunderstorm which left threatening skies and intense heat.

Madame Leonidov, lavishly swathed in silk, arrived early to take up her position under a group of palms in the hotel lounge. She and the Dowager Countess from Moscow were to act as hostesses.

When Charles came alone, in his heart prepared for the worst, he was pleasantly surprised to find himself in a crowd where it was possible to remain completely unnoticed. He could not even find Maria Ivanovna. He tried to make his way to the lower end of the long hall; but when a woman in a lace hat took his arm and, unaware that this unresisting limb did not belong to her husband, said, 'Oh, my dear, do look at that china dog,' he gave up the attempt and sought refuge by a pillar where at least he could stand still. Fragments of conversation, like pebbles thrown into a sea of air, reached him from all sides.

'If I had known that this bazaar was to do with Russians,' said a woman close to him, 'I wouldn't have come. My husband disapproves of Bolshevism. He did awfully badly with some shares during the War. He had to sell our new car.'

'These people aren't Bolsheviks, my dear,' said another voice. 'They are not in the least like the cartoons in *Punch*, those hairy men and bears and things. Just look at that woman with the diamonds and the marvellous yellow hair. She's not a Bolshy.'

'But, Joan, you always judge by appearances. They are probably all the same at heart. Anyway, they are Russians . . .' The speaker moved away and the rest of her remark was lost on Charles. He smiled to himself. Exactly what he thought. They were Russian; one couldn't tell with them. It sounded nice to call them versatile and gifted and one thing and another, but they were dashed unreliable!

He couldn't have said why without any direct cause he instinctively accused them of this. The opinion was part of his inherent prejudice against people who never did anything like anyone else.

The bazaar was doing well. Madame Leonidov, moving through the hall as though it were empty, surveyed the work of her hands with the satisfaction of a general who has taken risks in battle and secured victory. Her beautiful smile never left her face; her gleaming eyes sought and held glances directed at her arresting figure from every corner of the hall. She commanded attention, and she knew that when she passed people asked each other who 'the beautiful woman' was.

There was a slight flutter when the Governor's wife, a

little woman, rather half-heartedly conscious of the dignity of her position, arrived and was greeted by Madame Leonidov. She reported afterwards that Lady Mynge was charming and had made several intelligent remarks about Russia.

'These English ladies are quite well educated, you know. They appear so stupid only because they are so reserved,' was the verdict she passed.

It was, nevertheless, this harmless little lady's willingness to be entertained that shook Madame Leonidov's conviction that the dignity of her presence was sufficient in itself to ensure the success of any social function. Lady Mynge was pressed to stay and see the child dancer, who was to perform directly Madame Nikitin had ceased giving encores, and she stayed. Chairs had been placed in a semi-circle round the end of the hall free from stalls and palms, and the Governor's wife was escorted into the middle of the front row by Madame Leonidov and the Dowager Duchess. General Koubakin rallied those who had left their seats during the intervals in the singing, and commanded that the floor should be swept. Somebody hastened to remove all traces of dust and the child with her mother appeared through a side door. A gaunt woman in black sat down at the piano and struck the opening chords of a Chopin waltz. The child's first pirouette was greeted with applause, but the clapping died away rather suddenly. Something appeared to be wrong. There were signs of uneasiness in the front row. Charles, who was at the back and could see nothing but a pair of thin arms waving in time to a halting rendering of the waltz, poked the nearest familiar shoulder to ask what was wrong. No one seemed to know. At the end of the dance, which raised a few half-hearted claps, Koubakin came up to him. He was amused, and Charles could hardly follow the drift of his loud whispering interrupted by bursts of laughter which he considered subdued.

It appeared that the child was too scantily clothed, because the bodice of her yellow skirt was of transparent net – 'quite indecent,' Koubakin was saying. 'She is thirteen at least, I am sure. The mother ought to know better. The Governor's wife is shocked. Madame Leonidov is placed in a delicate position. These people are so inconsiderate. English, too, the modest English, the prudes. The mother is English, you see.' This fact that the mother was English seemed to delight him, because he went off into roars of laughter.

'Why on earth can't she go away and be done with it?' said Charles, determined to take no part in the joke.

'Oh, that would not help. The impression is created already. If the Governor's wife had not seen it, it would be most amusing; but she is shocked. The ladies in the front are so nervous they cannot sit still. Look at Elena Michailovna ! '

Charles looked. She had left her chair and was expostulating with the mother. The Dowager Countess had fixed her lorgnette on the girl, who, abashed by the cold stare of many eyes, fidgeted nervously with her skirt. Charles began to feel sorry for her and wished that she could hide herself from those rows of whispering, staring people. When at last she did run to her mother, he turned away so as not to witness the scene which he expected to follow.

He went to the bar, where several men were already discussing the incident. The news that something not quite nice had happened circulated through the crowd with a rapidity worthy of Koubakin's efforts to pass on the joke. On his way back into the hall Charles met Madame Leonidov.

'*Mon cher*, did you see?' she said, stopping him. 'It was terrible. Lady Mynge has gone, and of course she was most kind – but our reputation! How these English will talk about us poor Russians! I feel quite *compromise*. The hall is empty . . . already they are all going.'

'My dear Madame, you exaggerate. No one will think twice about this stupid business. And look at that crowd . . .' He pointed to a group of people near an empty stall. 'Besides, people would have started going anyhow. It's past six.'

She did not listen to him. 'I spoke to the mother. Of course she apologised and seemed ashamed, but she deserved my reprimand. So foolish of her, do you not think so?'

Charles left her and went to look for Maria Ivanovna. They went away without waiting for the hall to clear of its last visitors.

They walked for a while without speaking; then Maria Ivanovna said:

'I heard this afternoon that Homoutov is coming back.'

'Good God!' The words were out before he had time to stop himself. After a long pause he added, trying to sound casual:

'Who told you?'

'Vera. He wrote to Madame Leonidov. The letter was from Egypt, so that he will be here quite soon. But why are you so surprised?'

Vera! It *would* be Vera who announced what he had dreaded all these weeks. He slipped his arm through hers as if by this gesture to allay the suspicions he might have aroused. Not daring to look at her, he answered:

'I am not surprised, only you see he told me that he would be back in September at the earliest. In fact, I believe he did not intend to stop at Malta on his way to Europe. It's funny that he should change his plans like that; but we must just wait and see, I suppose.'

He did not have to wait long. Homoutov was a man who could overcome distance with greater speed than anyone else. He travelled without rest, preoccupied only with saving time. If he arrived an hour earlier than he was expected he was pleased; if he shortened his journey by a whole day he was exultant. This time his letter preceded him only by twenty-four hours, and the evening of the bazaar he appeared at the Villa.

When about nine o'clock he rang the bell, Madame Leonidov, exhausted, as she informed everyone, but wearing a look of self-satisfaction, had settled down to play patience. Koubakin was there, shouting out his impressions of the day to Abramovitch, who had appeared at the beginning of the afternoon, only to elbow his way out of the hall directly he had come in. Vera was about to count the money. Rows of cash boxes had been placed on a table by the window, and when she rose to answer the clanging bell a slight draught, caused by the opening of the door, made a piece of paper flutter from the table to the floor. Abramovitch stooped to pick it up. Perhaps because of what happened afterwards, perhaps because the others were intent listening to the voices outside and a hush had fallen on the room, he remembered that action all his life. Had his mind not been tinged with a delicate scepticism he might have seen something ominous in the importance he attached to such an insignificant thing as the ruffling of a sheet of paper in the draught. But his intellect was too sensitive to admit of superstition, and he was left to explain it as best he could.

Homoutov's figure in the doorway created a disturbance. Madame Leonidov almost rushed to meet him. Everyone talked at the same time. Even before they had sat down again, he made his usual present of lace and listened to the praises poured out by them with a modest yet self-assured air which conveyed very clearly the thoughts uppermost in his mind.

'Made by the native women, you know . . . Quite fine enough for Regent Street. . . . Notice the originality of this design . . . Look how beautifully this is executed. They are most talented . . . not at all undeveloped. My wife . . .' And so on till lack of breath would force him to stop. But this time he got no opportunity to talk. It was Madame Leonidov's voice which dominated the voices of the others.

'Petr Petrovitch, this is really too generous. A poor woman like myself doesn't expect such magnificent presents nowadays. There was a time. . . . But I adore lace. I always have adored it. I remember in Russia, when my husband wanted to give me diamonds, I would say: "Ivan Ivanovitch, I love diamonds – but give me lace." There is something so *fin*, so *distingué* about lace. You have really touched me.'

Homoutov bowed.

'And how is it that you are here so soon? You wonderful man, you are the true traveller; you go everywhere so quickly. But we only received your letter yesterday. I cannot understand it.'

'I did not wait for the boat at Suez. They were stopping there two days, so I went overland to Port Said – and here I am.'

When later they had settled down to tea, Homoutov asked after Maria Ivanovna. He always considered it his duty to mention anyone connected with the Villa and at that moment absent, just to show how friendly and amiable he was. Why did he not see her? Was she away? He hoped she wasn't ill.

'Why, of course, you don't know!' exclaimed Vera. 'She is married. She married quite soon after you went back to Madagascar. They live in Sliema.'

'How delightful! But . . . I don't remember anyone who . . . ?'

Madame Leonidov fixed him with her clear shining eyes.

'Your friend,' she said, in a meaning voice, as if she wanted to make him responsible for the actions of his friends. 'Mr Wilson has married her. It does not seem to me that they are happy. He is morose, *taciturne*, and she . . .' Her shoulders moved to express her inability to say anything at all definite about Maria Ivanovna.

Homoutov swallowed nothing several times. He felt as though someone had dropped a brick not quite heavy enough to stun him completely on his head.

'But, Elena Michailovna,' he said at last, 'what you say can't be true. He was married already. I know his wife. I met her in London.' He would have given a great deal to be able to go on speaking, but at that moment words failed him, and he could think of nothing else to say. He could not explain; he was as much at a loss as they were. At the back of his mind stirred the hope that he was dreaming or that they had lied. Madame Leonidov was the first to recover from dumb surprise. With an accusing, angry look, she said:

'I thought so! I told you so!' They all knew she had not, but not one of them could contradict her. They were too much astounded. Even Vera was silent, her features set in an expressionless smile which seemed to have frozen on her face. She kept her eyes on Houmoutov, making him fidget under her stare. Uneasily he shifted his feet, and Madame Leonidov, as if the scraping of his heels had reminded her that he was responsible for their anger and astonishment, turned on him.

'I cannot believe this, Petr Petrovitch. You are forgetting yourself, or else your friend is a criminal – *your friend*.' (She accented the words.) 'You introduced him here.'

'Believe me, Elena Michailovna, it is true. How could I know? I never thought of telling you he had a wife.'

'Anyway, who is she? Perhaps he can divorce her, make her keep quiet about it in some way.'

'He may want them both. You don't know the English, Elena Michailovna,' said Vera. Her ill-timed sarcasm provoked Madame Leonidov.

'Don't talk nonsense, my dear. I always knew you had no

principles. You don't seem to realise how serious it is. Think what a difficult position I am in. The girl lived with me for years; the man came to my house; and I am responsible for their marriage. What will everybody say? I shall be accused, of course, as I was accused of bringing that girl to dance this afternoon. The Governor's wife was not pleased, you know, Vera, to see naked – yes, naked – girls at the bazaar; and if it had not been for my tact our reputation would have been lost. Of course I explained, and the mother apologised; but we must first of all think of our reputation.'

'Her reputation,' put in Homoutov, because the thought that he had brought unhappiness and disgrace on the girl had already begun to torture him.

'Oh, she hadn't got any,' boomed Koubakin.

'I always said she was a fool and that you were too kind to her, Elena Michailovna. What did she want to marry that Englishman for? No one knew anything about him.'

'You are quite right, General,' answered Madame Leonidov; 'it is impossible to trust the English. But now what are we to do?'

Abramovitch looked up.

'Do? Why should you want to do anything? It is not your business.'

Madame Leonidov raised her hands as though to invoke angelic witnesses of this iniquity.

'I don't know if you ever think, but we are people who know the meaning of the word "morality". How can this sort of thing be left alone? It is the duty of every person – I do not say Christian, I always consider your views – to prevent such crimes. In the eyes of God it is a crime. In my eyes it is a crime. Your attitude is inexcusable. The world will not think as you do, and our reputation will be worth no more than that wretched girl's. You know how difficult life is for us. We are exiles: we have no country: we have no laws. We are at the mercy of foreigners who blame us for every scandal. Have you already forgotten Doctor Michailov's affair with Lidia Ivanovna? If it had not been for the efforts of people who like myself are devoted to the honour of Russia, it would never have been hushed up.' But she did not succeed in silencing Abramovitch.

'You mean,' he said, 'that if you and your friends had not spread false and abominable lies about it, Michailov might not have taken his own life. You have no right to talk about that, as you have no right to interfere here.'

For a moment Madame Leonidov looked as though she would choke. Her pale face turned a dull red, and the muscles of her neck swelled above the high, white-edged collar of her black dress. Homoutov edged further into his corner. Koubakin, reflecting that it was not often that he had such an amusing day as this one, turned his broad back on them and began to examine the miniatures on the mantelpiece. Vera only smiled.

'Abramovitch, you insult me,' cried Madame Leonidov, slapping the table with the palm of her hand. 'You who have lived on the money of a poor widow for more years than there are hairs on your head, you repay her kindness like this? There is gratitude for you, my friends!' She rose, gathering the folds of her dress about her, and when she had surveyed them in silence, added:

'I cannot bear it. I must grieve over this alone,' and

sailed from the room, pressing a handkerchief to her eyes.

When the sound of her footsteps had died away, Koubakin, still fingering the miniatures, said:

'Well, now what are we going to do? I must confess that your remarks to Elena Michailovna were most indiscreet. It is best to smooth these things over, you know.'

'Yes,' said Abramovitch dully. He lit a cigarette, but did not smoke it. Vera looked at him angrily, because she always insisted that smoke was bad for her lungs. No one had ever interfered with the delusion except Abramovitch, who, she declared, always behaved as if she, Vera, were not there.

Koubakin turned round and, putting his hands with fingers outstretched behind his back as if he were shielding it from an imaginary fire in the grate, addressed the others with the ponderous gravity he assumed on the least occasion.

'Somebody must speak to him. He must be warned that if he does not decide on a definite course of action we shall adopt legal proceedings.' He looked round for approval. 'You understand me. I mean – legal proceedings. I shall be very firm about this. I insist that the law be used to intimidate him.'

'Boris Ephraimovitch, I don't suppose he will want intimidating. He is as great a coward as any of that mean race of shopkeepers. It's the woman . . .' Vera gave them a dark, ominous look.

'Oh, Vera Antonovna, this is unjust. Poor Maria Ivanovna, it is not her fault! And she is such a charming girl, so good-natured.'

Homoutov spoke appealingly, as though he wanted them all to agree on the subject of Maria Ivanovna's good nature.

'I warned her,' continued Vera, taking no notice of him. 'I never trusted that man for a moment, especially after meeting that officer who said he knew a Charles Wilson who was married. It was on the day of the wedding, too.'

This was untrue. She had not thought about the officer until then; but she knew it would impress them.

'I wonder who he was,' muttered Homoutov.

Koubakin, feeling that the conversation was passing out of his hands, interposed.

'All this is not to the point, my friends. With all due respect to you, Vera Antonovna, I must say that it does not matter now what you thought. We must not think; we must act. I have already told you that the man must be spoken to. If you agree, I am ready to do it myself. As a general, and a fitting representative of the Russian colony in Malta, I will take this responsibility on myself. I will shield the girl.'

He expanded his chest and paused for their assent. But Abramovitch, whom he had thought asleep, so motionless had he sat with an unsmoked cigarette burning itself out between his fingers, Abramovitch, whom he despised more than any man he knew, contradicted him. Heaving his thin, loose-limbed body up from the sofa, as if he realised that the time had come for action, he said, looking down his thin nose at Koubakin, who was short and hated tall men:

'Mr Wilson and I have been on friendly terms together. Homoutov, too, is his friend. We will do what is necessary.'

'Quite right, quite right,' said Homoutov. 'Of course we will do what we can. My dear General, leave it to us;

Abramovitch and I will be tactful.'

Koubakin did not reply. His face wore a look of pity and contempt for the fools who prevented a man from doing what obviously he alone could do. At last, when he had several times breathed heavily down his beard, he said:

'As my presence is no longer required, I will take my leave. Vera Antonovna, good night.'

He went out and Vera followed him.

When the door shut behind them Abramovitch, left standing in the middle of the floor, did not even look at Homoutov. He went up to the table and poured himself out a cup of cold tea. Homoutov, anxious to put an end to the silence, began to speak in a nervous voice.

'I am terribly upset. I don't know what to think. I cannot believe it. There must be some mistake.'

Abramovitch pushed aside his cup and got up.

'They have gone,' he said. 'I will see you out. Believe me, there is no mistake except this – we imagine that we are free, but because we are cowards we can never find our freedom.'

Homoutov did not ask him what he meant. Somehow it did not seem to matter.

VIII

WHEN, A FEW DAYS AFTER Homoutov's arrival, Charles
ran into Abramovitch in the street, he knew at once that he
could no longer avoid the conversation for which he had
been prepared since Homoutov's visit. He had come to see
him, but had gone away without saying anything. In the
silent, nervous man who found it difficult to make the most
ordinary remarks, Charles could hardly recognise the cheerful, loquacious Homoutov, complacent, and in spite of
increasing years still known as 'young'. He had found it difficult enough to keep up a conversation alone with Charles;
but his wits failed him completely when Maria Ivanovna
came in.

She greeted him with an animation which surprised him
because he had never noticed it before; and overcome by
confusion at hearing her laugh and talk, unconscious of the
fact that he had come to destroy her happiness, he fled with
a broken excuse.

He confessed to Abramovitch that it had been like moving in a nightmare.

'God knows I am not a serious man,' he said, but I have

always been honest. I have remained faithful to my wife in Madagascar. This is too much for me to understand.'

When Charles caught sight of Abramovitch's tall, stooping figure in the street, he kept his head turned away until he felt a hand on his shoulder.

'I was coming to you,' Abramovitch said. 'Are you busy?'

No,' replied Charles, unable to think of an excuse.

'Let's go in there, then.' He pointed to a teashop across the road.

They went in. It was dark and the place was almost deserted. Several untidy girls stood about in bored attitudes; and at a table near the window sat a woman with two fair-haired children. She was well-groomed, assertive, and obviously English. She gave Charles a long look from under a large white hat, but turned away when she had noticed Abramovitch with his dusty trousers and shapeless coat. They sat down and ordered tea. For a while neither spoke. Charles fidgeted with his spectacles and Abramovitch was absorbed in the fate of a fly which struggled helplessly in some milk spilt on the marble top of the table. When he had saved it and with a straw dried its sticky wings, he said:

'You saw Homoutov yesterday? You know why I want to speak to you?'

The spectacles made a scratchy noise on the table. This was more absurd than anything he had ever imagined. Angry at being trapped, and clutching desperately for the last shreds of his respectability, he took up an offensive attitude.

'Yes, and I should like to know why you all come round interfering with me and my affairs. What business have you to believe what Homoutov or any other man says about me? It has nothing to do with you.'

Abramovitch remained unperturbed. When later Charles remembered this scene, it struck him that Abramovitch had spoken and behaved as if he had had a fixed idea which nothing that was said or done could in any way alter. He seemed to be reaching out to some thought, disconnected from anything which might be in the mind of the person whom he addressed, and whom he never allowed to interfere with the words 'but this is not true of *me*'.

'You would not have avoided me today,' he said, 'if Homoutov had not been right. Besides, why deny it? I don't accuse you. I am too old to accuse. I only want to help you.'

'Help me!' thought Charles bitterly. 'As if anybody ever wanted to or could do that.' But he did not answer. Abramovitch leant across the table. He was so near him that Charles could see the puffy wrinkles on his eyelids and the thin, black hairs which grew round his nostrils. He spoke slowly, in a low voice, as if every word cost him a great effort.

'I want to warn you,' he said. 'We were all in the drawing-room that night when Homoutov came. They know, and so will everybody unless you take care. Remember you are English; and because they hate and despise the English they will do everything in their power to ruin you. They love scandal, and they would not spare one of themselves for the pleasure of talking. It is as dear to them as their life. This is such a small place; they have so little to do. They will make you suffer. For Maria Ivanovna's sake you must do something.'

'What do you want me to do?' Charles spoke sullenly.

'I don't know . . . you could go away.' He seemed uncertain of himself now, anxious to avoid saying what was on his mind.

'You could get a divorce, I suppose . . . in England . . . marry her again.'

Charles hardly listened to what Abramovitch was saying. The words 'divorce', 'England', 'marry' reached him bereft of their meaning. His memory, which in those days of suspense he had kept closed to the past, had suddenly played him false. An image, torturing him with its reality, crept into his blank, tired mind. He saw Maria Ivanovna as he had seen her on that day when she had met him outside the door of the Villa, with Irochka's broken doll in her hands. He could not think of that day without emotion and regret. How they had wandered in those flowering fields! How absorbed they had been in their happiness! But first she had taken the doll indoors and put it away. Its skull was cracked and it had stupid glass-bright eyes. This thing came into his mind with the force of a blow from a hammer. He saw as clearly as if he had no part in the tragedy how utterly he had wrecked not only his own life, but hers. Pity, untouched with selfish fear, filled his heart with a bitter sense of futility and shame. She had been wonderful, unsullied by the ugliness of suffering, and he had loved her for her beauty and her strength. And now what had he done? In her turn she was broken and, like the doll with unseeing, staring eyes, would be hidden away, unfortunate, unpitied.

Abramovitch was stirring his tea with a spoon. A streak of light penetrated through the skylight window and lay, a path of dust, between the ceiling and the floor.

'Well,' Charles said at last, 'I suppose you are right. But you must think me a damned rotter. I don't know why you speak to me.'

'For the woman's sake,' replied Abramovitch. 'Why should she suffer because of you? You have sacrificed her to your desire, and now you can think only of yourself. Oh, I know what you are going to say; I understand you perfectly; I am a Jew. I have no life of my own. It is long since I ceased to care for myself, and instead have watched the lives of others. That is why I am speaking to you when others wouldn't. I don't blame you. Like all of us, you have been defeated by your ideals. You wanted something different; you were sick of yourself, of the life you led year after year tied to a dull past which was like a chain dragging you back from your future. You wanted to get away from your own mediocrity and turn from the mean things round you. You thought you would find all you sought in this woman: you loved her for the sake of the happiness you could not attain alone. And when it seemed to you that your life depended on her – and when you were afraid to lose your life in losing her – you let yourself be mastered by your fear and you ruined yourself by your cowardice. It is always like that. We are all cowards when our happiness is at stake. We try to cheat and steal a march on life; but we can't, you know. Look at me. I did the same, only I loved the woman more for her own sake than for mine, but it made no difference. I was worn out by the longings which we sometimes call ideals, but which are no more than a desire for happiness. After all, it is easy to be dissatisfied; it is natural to want

141

something better; but it is the effort of getting it which breaks us. We are not strong enough. We do not realise our weakness until it is too late. It is perhaps impossible that we should. But the worst of it is, isn't it, that we are defeated through our own fault? We like to call it "circumstances" when we have not the courage to acknowledge our own weakness. We talk of "fate", but we have our fate in our own hands.'

He broke off and leant back wearily in his chair. Charles, wholly occupied by his own thoughts, could find nothing to say to him. In the end, all this talk was just waste of time – it did neither of them any good. He decided he had better go before Abramovitch started off again.

'Well, thank you very much,' he said in a precise, matter-of-fact voice as though their conversation had been of the most ordinary kind. 'I am very grateful to you, but I think perhaps I had better go home. My wife . . .' He stopped. Abramovitch bowed over the table.

'I apologise for speaking to you like this. I quite realise – your private affairs. But I am sincerely interested. You have my sympathy, and Maria Ivanovna,' he smiled, 'is a charming person. She deserves to be happy. If you let me know what you decide I will inform our friends. It needs tact – you understand me?'

'Oh, quite. Goodbye.' Charles picked up his hat and went out. Looking round at the door, he saw him sitting, his elbows on the table, his head in his hands: a thin, dark figure a little bent at the shoulders, a little pitiful to look at.

Driven to the point of action, partly by the fear of scandal, partly by the desire to be free from the uncertainty which had weighed on him so long, Charles decided to leave Malta as soon as possible. The pity which Abramovitch's words and his own memories had wakened in him for Maria Ivanovna did not leave him. He accused himself of having neglected her and repaid her love with callous indifference. Abramovitch was right. He had thought only of himself. He was determined now that whatever happened she should not suffer for his sake. He would go back to England, divorce Lucy, and she need never know. Lucy would set him free when she knew everything. She would not break her heart over him. He did not know much about divorce cases, but he imagined that Maria's name could be passed over. Besides, she never read the papers. All this seemed so simple to him now, that he was surprised that he had not acted before and had wasted so much time in idle conjecture and fears. He had treated her badly too; he had resented her presence as a man resents the presence of those he has wronged. He had accused her of being dull and unexpansive when his sullen ill-humour had driven her to seek refuge in a passive silence with which she screened herself from his egoism. He determined that in the last days they spent together he would allow nothing to mar their happiness.

She had taken the news of his departure with a calm which relieved and at the same time astonished him. She seemed resigned that he should leave her, as though she had been prepared for this change in their life. She showed no grief or astonishment.

He found it easy to fulfil the promise he gave himself to

make her happy at least for this short while. He again fell under the spell of her beauty, which revived with his tenderness and filled him with compassion that he had so nearly sacrificed her to his selfish cowardice. He treasured her every word, her least gesture, and vowed to himself that nothing would separate her from him.

They lived in feverish impatience of every moment spent in each other's arms, as though they were on the edge of an abyss into which they would be precipitated as the hours and days grew into weeks. The time for his departure grew nearer and she became more restless. One day he found her in tears, kneeling before an open trunk, with his clothes in untidy piles around her. There was something hopeless in the obstinate silence of her grief. When he asked her what had so suddenly upset her, she only shook her head, and, trying to hide her tear-stained face from him, began to throw into the trunk the things she had been holding on her lap. He tried to console her, but, troubled by her distress, he found it hard to sound convincing. After all, did he not know far less than she did what he would find when he was in London? Words failing him, he took her into his arms and kissed her; but he felt uneasy under the scrutiny of her eyes.

'You are not leaving me for ever?' she said at last, when he raised his face from hers. 'You will come back? I don't know what is making me so afraid. I must be mad.'

He answered her lightly.

'Why, of course. It is only for a short time, you know. And if I don't come back, you will come to me. You won't mind going to England, will you?'

'No, I will wait as long as you like if you write. You promise you love me always? You promise not to forget – oh, I know you cannot, you will not forget.' She put her hand to her mouth as though to stifle a moan, and ran to the door. Surprised and a little irritated, Charles could only say:

'My dear, you must be calm. Do control yourself.' But she did not hear him: she had gone: and when a moment later he went to look for her, he found her composed, and anxious to excuse herself for what she called her 'nerves'. She blamed the heat and the strain of packing his trunks, and he allowed himself to be reasoned out of his uneasiness for her.

She did not break down again. Abramovitch, who took her back from the harbour to the empty, disordered flat, after Charles had gone, wondered at the strength of this woman whose spirit seemed undaunted by grief.

'She bears things well,' he thought, 'but then how much of it all has she to bear?'

IX

FOR A WHILE his letters came to her frequently. He kept his promise. He wrote short monosyllabic notes, telling her how much he loved her, and how soon he would make her join him in London. He was never eloquent. He did not know how to express what he felt in letters, and the tender words which flow easily from lovers came to him with an effort. He laboured over his sentences like a schoolboy over an exercise; he turned out clauses in which the emotion he tried to express was like a glue used to stick together their stiff joints.

She did not mind, however. She treasured his untidy scrawls and answered him with many pages covered in neat, thin writing. When his letters became less frequent, hers filled in the intervals. She did not resent his long silences, because she told herself that he was busy making preparations for their life together in England, and that soon he would tell her to come to him.

She waited through August and September, patient, and never doubting his good faith. The last week of September brought her no news. She did not despair, but wrote almost daily. Towards the end of October, looking back over the dreary period of silence, she realised that perhaps she would hear no more and fear assailed her.

She had lived on the reserves of patience and endurance which through long, colourless years had accumulated within her, but her strength was at last beginning to wear out. She suffered terribly when twice a day she watched the postman wander along the street, come up to the door of the house, and leave his letters. She would run downstairs, examine letter after letter, and when she had dropped the last envelope, which for the space of a few hours killed her hopes, she could hardly summon enough strength to mount the steep flights of stairs to her flat at the top of the house. She would drag her feet up wearily, taking long rests on the landings, unaware that people who passed her often wondered at the pallor of her face and the look of suffering which darkened her eyes.

She lived alone except for a woman who came to help her. She was of a bright, kind nature, and lavish in her sympathy for the young signora because she was unhappy and had no news from her husband. Except for this woman, with whom she talked Italian and English interspersed with as much Maltese as she knew, Maria Ivanovna saw no one. Earlier in the autumn, and when letters still came from Charles, she had paid a visit to the Villa.

She was received with a coldness for which she had not been prepared, although she knew she could expect but little from them. Madame Leonidov stared at her as though surprised and annoyed that she should be there, and after remarking laconically:

'Well, and how are you?' sent Irochka to play by herself in the garden. 'It is bad for you to be always with grown-ups,' she had said.

From her Maria Ivanovna turned to Homoutov, in the hope that he would be glad to talk to her, but he had been silent and ill at ease. Alone Abramovitch had been glad to see her and had shaken himself out of his taciturnity to make her feel that at least she was welcomed by him. But she knew that in taking notice of her he displeased Madame Leonidov, and she had not returned to the Villa.

Once, shortly after that visit, she met Vera in the street.

'Oh, my dear,' she had said, taking Maria's hand between hers, 'how ill you look. Is anything the matter?'

'No, nothing.'

'Of course, with a young wife one never knows' – this with a deep affected significance – 'but Elena Michailovna is quite distressed that you never come to the Villa. Although you are married' – again the slight emphasis and the pause – 'you should not forget your friends, you know.'

'I am so busy,' pleaded Maria Ivanovna. 'I have to get ready to go to England.' She lied bravely. Nothing could have forced her secret from her, made her betray herself and her husband. She hoped that this lie would satisfy Vera. After all, was anything more natural than that she should follow him? But her curiosity only seemed to increase.

'So you are going?' she said, speaking very quickly, as though she were afraid Maria Ivanovna might slip away before she had finished. 'How very unexpected! We did not think it would be so soon. But we shall miss you so much in this stupid little place! Madame Leonidov will be sad when she hears you are going. Forgive an old friend' – she squeezed the passive hand she still held – 'but I think you do not realise Elena Michailovna's affection for you. She thinks of you so often. She is so anxious for your happiness, as anxious as she would be for Irochka's. And all this time you have neglected us! I have heard her say so often, "Why doesn't Maria come? She is forgetting us poor Russians now that she has an English husband!"'

'She did not seem pleased to see me when I came.' She felt nettled. The conversation was taking a turn she liked even less than Vera's questions. She knew it was her habit to accuse others of the shortcomings which were above all her own.

'Nor did any of you,' she added, a little resentfully.

'But, my dear, you must not think that. You know so well that we always leave our guests to entertain themselves. You are still one of us, although your husband is English. Don't forget to come soon. Homoutov is going to London before November, so perhaps you will go together.'

She left Maria Ivanovna with this thrust, and her delight in her own malice sent her hurrying back to the Villa, so that she might make much of the encounter before its significance became overshadowed in her mind by other matters of a like nature. Vera never went anywhere without meeting someone, and that someone never failed to impart to her the information she wanted. Her solicitude for her friends was always attributed to the generosity of her nature. It was generally agreed that she had 'the heart of an angel, and such a charming way of putting things'.

Meanwhile Maria Ivanovna was left to puzzle over the

hidden meaning of Vera's remarks and wonder what provoked the hostility she felt in Madame Leonidov's cold looks and in Vera's inquisitiveness. She had never liked or trusted them, but she had never before been driven to grapple with the problem of the motives which lay behind their actions. When there had been no explanation she had sought none, taking refuge in the instinctive pessimism common to many sensitive natures. But now their attitude assumed a greater importance in her eyes. They became to her an unknown evil power, opposing her and driving her into doubt and grief. Her mind groped helplessly in the impenetrable mist of ignorance which she felt clinging round her. She tried to meet despair with reason and argue herself into sanity. But every day it seemed to her that she walked further into a bog which gave way under her feet and sucked her under the ground. A nameless terror surged up from the depths of her being. She could do nothing to banish it. It grew with every hour she spent alone, wandering about her rooms, sitting by the window, watching the sunlight move slowly round the house and creep up the walls, till at sunset its last rays glowed upon the dirty window panes. Sometimes when that fear, which dulled her heartache, making her listen to the sound of her own footsteps and start at every noise in the street, when it rose and choked her with a sudden spasm of agony, she would try to master it by prayer. With his help she had hung up her icons in one corner of the room. She would stand for hours before them, repeating the words she had used since she was a child, and looking up at the dark, placid faces which seemed to stare relentlessly into her unseeing eyes.

She strove to occupy herself with such familiar, mechanical actions, because if she remained idle she thought only of her husband, and saw again and again the images which always recurred and paralysed her mind with their monotony. She had lost her grasp of what was vital and important. It was as if she had returned from a long journey and could describe nothing of it except the least details: the colour of the labels on her trunks, the number of her taxi, and how much she had tipped the porter at the station. Thus she could not remember her lover's face, the way he spoke and behaved. Only the negligible but familiar features of his person were stamped on her mind: the mole on his left cheek, the pink, transparent tips of his ears which grew red when he was angry or embarrassed; his peculiar stammer; the fact that he bought collars too large for him so that his neck looked thinner than it was. She had often teased him about this.

'Charles, I wish you would get collars the right size. These make you look like an inquisitive bird,' she would say, and he always replied:

'But, love, there is no right size for me.'

Such memories, stupid and insignificant, were invariably associated with her last recollection of him. She was afraid of them and tried to banish them from her mind, but she could not. For if ever she tried to think of his love and tenderness, every circumstance of it escaped her, and her heart ached at a void filled only by these persistent images which obscured her mind and tortured her by their reality. She felt that if she could remember how he had loved her she would regain her belief in his faithfulness to her. If only she could reach back through that endless stretch of days crowded with futile hopes! If only she could keep alive within her the innumerable signs of his love, the hours of passionate happiness, the tender words he lavished on her.

But every trace of this was lost to her. She could only ponder over the meaningless, vain things, which by a trick of her memory remained as the landmarks of her life with him.

The autumn rains had come with the last weeks of October. The fields were growing green after the long drought, but it was a dull, lifeless green, hardly visible through the mists which rose from the sea and wrapped the island in windless quiet. The towns had emptied of visitors and relapsed into the half-dormant state which came when the bustle and activity of European life was withdrawn from them. Maltese and Jews lounged about the streets. Foghorns echoed the church bells, and the familiar cry of 'Hali-ib' came through the rain like a Mussulman's mournful call to prayer. Slowly Malta was settling to the idle melancholy of a Mediterranean winter.

As the summer vanished Maria Ivanovna grew more afraid. Every day seemed to cut her off farther from the hope of seeing Charles again. She could not still the terror which filled her at the thought of long winter months, spent in waiting for the hours to pass, from morning till the time when she lit her lamp, from the moment when its white light first shone on the floor till the next dawn. The beating of the rain against her windows drove her out of doors, and she would wander in the empty streets and along the road which stretched out from Sliema to St Julian, and beyond to St Paul's Bay. She knew every corner of it, every bend which concealed or brought her nearer to the sea.

Once when she was on her way home and, tired out, could only move with difficulty in her stiff wet garments, she saw Abramovitch coming towards her. She tried to pass him, but he stopped her.

'How are you?' he said, looking at her with deep concern, as though to explain that he knew it was a useless question. She forced a smile to her pale lips.

'Quite well, but I am not looking forward to a lonely winter.' Her voice shook a little, but she kept her smile.

'Malta is dreadful then, isn't it? I hate the winds because I am not strong enough to climb about on the rocks when a gale is blowing.' He looked down apologetically at his thin bony knees. 'And you know how lost I am without my walks.'

At last she had summoned the courage to look into his face. Drops of rain glistened on his untidy beard. There was a large drop on the end of his thin, purple-veined nose. A strand of hair had stuck to his forehead. To anyone else he would at that moment have seemed ridiculous and a little pathetic, but to her there was something so gentle, so protecting in the kindliness of his small brown eyes and his smile, that before she realised what she was doing she had seized his damp red hand in hers and cried out:

'Where is my husband? Do you know what has happened to him?' Then, ashamed of herself, she turned away.

'I am sorry,' she said; 'I am sorry.'

He took her arm and led her down the street, because

they had attracted the attention of some dirty children, who left their games in the gutter and surrounded them with loud remarks and demands for pennies. They stopped in a doorway, which gave them a little shelter from the rain.

Without waiting for her to speak, he said:

'I know as little as you do. He told me he would return.' He was going to add something else, but did not. If she did not know why Charles had gone, was it his business to tell her? – Perhaps. But he could not do it now. He did not know how she would take it. She might faint. He would never get her home if a crowd of Maltese collected round them. He glanced at her face. It bore no traces of the suffering which a moment ago had contracted her features into a pitiful grimace.

'Let me take you home,' he said. 'It is bad for you to stand here in the rain. You must be wet through.'

Involuntarily he looked at her shoes. The soles were thin and the leather old. With a pang he realised that she was probably in need of money. She might even be starving in that empty flat. They had never thought of her at the Villa; they had neglected her for months.

When they reached the door of her house he detained her. A little nervous, but determined to carry out his intention, he muttered:

'Maria Ivanovna, I am an old friend. If you need anything, perhaps you would tell me. . . . I have a little that I have saved – my contributions to geological magazines, you know,' he added, as though in apology for his secret wealth. She rewarded him with her old smile. For one moment her face recaptured from it the light which was so peculiarly her

154

own, and which he had not expected to see again, because the severe look in her eyes seemed to forbid it. She gave him her hand and he kissed it, with an involuntary shiver, for as he bent his head the raindrops, which had gathered in a shining ridge on his coat collar, trickled down his neck.

'I shall not forget your kindness,' she said. 'You are the only friend I have left now.'

When the door had closed behind her he remained gazing at the spot where she had stood. So her charm was still the same! The beauty, which he had often watched quivering on her face like a gleam of light, was then not withered by those dreary months of waiting. He mused on the unstudied grace of her movements, the elusive way in which she had disappeared before he could call her back.

'Like a spirit,' he said to himself, as he carefully stepped into the pools of water which lay on the pavement. 'Silent and quick, like a spirit.'

He would have been surprised to know that it was he who had revived her beauty, kindled the life within her and brought back the old smile to her grave face. He saw her as she had been; he could not see her now walk up the stairs as if every step caused her pain, lean heavily against the banisters, pause wearily on every landing.

He went home resolved to speak to Madame Leonidov of her needs. But he found her unwilling to listen to him and full of her own cares, which she paraded for his benefit.

She was put upon by everybody, she complained; there was not one person she knew who did not want something or other from her. They all imagined she was rich. Just because she was careful and did not squander the little money she had, people thought she could afford to keep all the refugees in Malta. Only this afternoon Kondratieff had been to ask her to help him to send that wretched little boy of his to school Of course she had been very sorry for *'cette pauvre Sophie'*. Her tender heart always led her into difficulties, but he had made a scene when she refused. He said that they would starve; that he could earn so little. She had been most upset about it; her nerves were shaken; and now he, Abramovitch, only made it worse by telling her of that girl's difficult position. What had she to do with it?

'Think for yourself,' she said. 'What business is it of mine? I had to face the risk of a scandal. It was my painful duty to satisfy the inquiries of nearly everyone we know; and now, when the affair is safely over, you want *me* to help the abandoned wife and maintain her, instead of that abominable wretch who had the impudence to deceive us. This is a decent house, you know. I must think of the reputation of my daughter, if not of my own. You have no consideration for me. You never think of my nerves and my health.'

She began to cry, and Abramovitch hurriedly left the room. He knew that her tears were more inexorable than her words, and he decided to do without her help. He took out the few banknotes which lined his old wallet and sent them to Maria Ivanovna. They were returned the next day. She wrote that she did not need money; that she was grateful to him; and that if later she found herself in difficulties she would turn to him. After that there was nothing for him to do but wait till time should show what it reserved for her.

Unexpectedly for everyone, the weather suddenly changed. A warm wind had blown away the rain, and there was a short return of summer. The sun shone all day in a sky scattered with pale clouds which hung like flakes of mist over its brilliant surface. The sea was calm. The warmth called out loiterers into the streets; the dogs and the children crept out of their hiding-places and wallowed in the hot dust of the roads. The last flowers appeared in the fields; thin grass and hardy weeds struggled over the bare ground. Towards evening midges danced in the air. It was the Martinmas of the South, short-lived and deceptive.

They were glad at the Villa that it was warm again. The house was draughty and cold in the winter and the garden afforded them no protection but that of a few bushes whose skeleton-like branches writhed helplessly in the wind. But now the flaming nasturtium still straggled over the neglected flower-beds; and the mountain ash, which had grown up no one knew how at the end of the lawn, was hung with a few last bunches of red berries. Madame Leonidov declared that it reminded her of Russia, and made Vera carry the tea-tray beneath its branches. There she entertained her visitors, and there they sat and talked, a little more uncomfortable on the garden chairs than they used to be on the furniture of the drawing-room.

One evening, when besides Vera and Abramovitch only Homoutov was there, the conversation turned to Charles and Maria Ivanovna. It began with Homoutov's remark that he would be going to England quite soon. He had a great deal of lace to sell.

'Of course one does not know,' said Madame Leonidov,

'but it is quite possible that she may have a child. What will she do then? I really cannot imagine.'

She spoke in a voice which conveyed very clearly that she made no effort at all to imagine anything so unpleasant. Whenever she thus showed her indifference, Abramovitch felt wounded by it, as if it affected a person very dear to him, instead of one who, in spite of the long years he had known her, was almost a stranger. He decided to make another effort to enlist their sympathy.

'I don't think she knows why he left her,' he said, and paused to see what effect his words had on them. There was a curious expression he did not like on Vera's face.

'Doesn't know!' she exclaimed. 'It seems to me that your admiration for her makes you talk rubbish. Why, if he didn't tell her, I expect a thousand people have. What about Koubakin for one? How many times, do you think, has he expressed his sympathy? I myself have always made it quite clear to her that I understood her position perfectly.'

Homoutov, who whenever Maria Ivanovna was mentioned felt guilty and embarrassed, moved uneasily in his chair. He hated arguments, and besides, one never knew where one was with Vera Antonovna. She was an excellent girl, he had no doubt – but such a tongue! Madame Leonidov, anxious to dispel his uneasiness, remarked that of course she was sorry for the poor girl, especially if she did not know, but then what could one do? Who could tell her such a monstrous thing? And to show how deeply she felt the monstrosity of it, she sighed and gazed a little pensively at the sea.

'How calm it looks,' she murmured, after a suitable

interval of silence. 'The end of November – one would not think it.'

The next day was very hot, and Vera, as she set out from the Villa, thought that there was thunder in the air. Quite probably this heavy, listless atmosphere presaged a storm. After all, the fine weather could not last. So, ignoring the fact that the sky was cloudless, she took an umbrella. She hated getting wet – besides, it spoilt one's hats. She hurried all the way into Sliema, as though afraid that rain or something unforeseen would stop her; and she was out of breath when she reached the house where Maria Ivanovna lived. She had been there once, soon after the marriage, and had thought the hired furniture vulgar. She was let into the flat by the cheerful Maltese girl, who recognised her and said that although the signora saw visitors very rarely she would be pleased . . . Vera cut her short and herself opened the door of the only sitting-room. It was small and rather dark. There was a mirror on the wall opposite the windows, a sofa covered with ugly green material, one or two thin-legged tables, and a few chairs. Maria Ivanovna was sitting by the open window and at first did not notice her. When in answer to Vera's exclamation she rose and turned, it seemed to Vera that she had aged since she had last seen her. There was a heavy, dull look about her, peculiar to the faces of those who rarely sleep, and her hands were restless. It was obvious that she made efforts to keep them still.

She seemed quite glad to see Vera and thanked her warmly for the untidy bunch of late chrysanthemums that Vera had picked for her in the garden. But she did not trouble to get water for them, merely putting them down on a table, by the side of a small jar of thick yellow glass in which there were a few chocolates. They talked a little about their acquaintances, and then Vera asked:

'When are you going to England?'

Maria Ivanovna's face reddened slightly.

'Oh, I don't know. Not very soon,' she replied. Vera sat forward in her chair. She always liked to sit on the very edge of a chair; it gave her confidence.

'I suppose you have not heard from your husband?' She smiled a bright and cheerful smile which was meant to confirm the impression that of course she was only asking an ordinary question; but she did not take her eyes from Maria Ivanovna's face. She watched her teeth close on her lower lip, and saw the involuntary, convulsive movement of her hand with the thin gold ring on one finger.

'Why do you talk about my husband?' she said at last in a low voice.

'Oh, nothing.' Vera looked out of the window. The sky was grey.

'It's going to rain,' she thought. 'I am glad I brought that umbrella. I can now stay here as long as I like.'

'What is the matter with you, Vera?' She heard Maria Ivanovna's voice close to her, and, turning her head away from the window, saw that she was leaning forward in her chair, her hands clasped on her knee.

'Why do you come here and torture me like this? What are you trying to conceal from me? I know it is something. What is it?'

Her voice was calm, but there was something in the way she spoke which made Vera feel uneasy. She tried to sound very casual.

'Oh, it is all right – only I thought you knew, you poor thing.'

With these last words all her patience and good nature and kindness broke down. She hadn't come here to sympathise and console. She obeyed another impulse than that of pity. Once more composed, she waited for an answer. After a long silence it came.

'Knew? Knew what?'

Directly the words had passed her lips she understood that she had given herself away, but she could no longer think clearly. Something tightened beneath her breast. The terror against which she had struggled so long leaped at her fiercely. Her knees shook and she could see nothing but two circles of light dancing before her eyes, intertwining like headless serpents.

'I think I had better go. I am sorry I have upset you.' She heard the voice, muffled and faint as though coming from very far away. Then the thought flashed through her mind that she must not let that voice go; that if it became silent now it would leave her straining to hear it, deaf for ever to every other sound.

'No,' she said, standing up, as if by that action she could force the voice to continue speaking.

'You must not go now. Tell me what you know.' And after a pause she added: 'Have pity on me. Don't leave me like this.' The pain she felt at her breast hindered her from speaking in a loud voice. She felt that she had not enough breath left in her body to make herself heard. Her last words came out in a hoarse whisper.

Vera watched her. She had not thought her victory would be so easy. At last this woman whom she hated was humbled, disgraced, supplicating and entreating her without a shred of pride to clothe her shame. A wild desire to laugh came over her. She wanted to laugh so that not only Maria would hear her, but the maid in the kitchen and all the people in the street. She wanted to fill the room, the whole house, with the sound of it; to shake the walls and see them toppling about her, shattered like this woman was shattered, by the power of her mirth. But she controlled herself with the thought that she was growing hysterical, and only shrugged her shoulders.

'Well, why are you silent?'

She could not help shrinking from Maria's eyes, but she mastered her fear and replied:

'I don't know what you want of me or why you are making such a fuss. Of course, we would have told you before, but how could we imagine that you would never guess that the man you call your husband had a wife when he married you?'

She had spoken slowly, feeling that the deliberation with which her lips formed each word turned it into a weapon.

Maria Ivanovna did not move. She was standing up very straight as if trying to see something just above Vera's head, her mouth distended in a smile. Somehow that expressionless smile roused her anger, and, seizing Maria's wrist, she said very quickly and almost under her breath:

'Stop smiling, you little fool. What are you smiling at? Have you got another lover that you are glad to be rid of that one?'

Then she laughed, but the laugh which came from her throat was thin and high, more like a whining sob than a laugh. She tried to stop, but she could not. She went on making that noise which sounded so terrible in her own ears, till her whole body shook with it.

Maria Ivanovna did not look at her. She walked to the table and slowly lifted the cover off the yellow glass bowl. As she did so her sleeve caught the flowers and they fell, scattering their thin petals, white streaked with purple, on the floor. She did not heed them, but took a chocolate out of the bowl, bit it, and as though revolted by its taste, quickly put it down on the table. Choking back her laughter, Vera watched her. They were so close to each other that when Maria bent her head she could see a faint yellowish line of dirt round the neck of her blouse. Without turning round, slowly she walked to the door in that corner of the room where stood the green sofa, and opened it. It shut so quietly behind her that Vera gasped to hear the turn of the lock. The creaking of a chair reached her through the thin wall and then there was silence.

For a moment she stood not knowing what to do; then she picked up the flowers, laid them on the table, and replaced the cover of the glass bowl. She crossed the room on tiptoe and, opening the door into the hall, listened, but she heard no sound, and, shutting the door carefully behind her, she fled. She ran down the narrow stairs and out of the street door.

Without even looking round, she ran through narrow, evil-smelling alleys where she had never been before. Unaware that the patch of sky visible above the roofs was the colour of lead, and that she had forgotten her umbrella, she pushed her way through groups of lounging people who stared after her. A man seized her by the arm, but she wrenched it free and ran on, stumbling over stones, falling over her skirt. She did not stop till she had passed the last houses of the town. Then, when she was beyond all shelter, the storm broke over her head.

Every thunder clap seemed to her the last she would hear before the clouds were hurled like mountains on the earth. The lightning now plunged like a sharp flame into the sea, now danced upon the roof of some house, or among the tops of the cowering trees. She ran on, the wind screaming about her ears. Gusts of rain drove her forward, blinding her. She had lost the road and was clambering over walls and ditches, tearing her way through coarse, wet grass which whipped her legs. At last she came to the edge of a cliff. When the thunder was silent she could hear the beating of the waves. The rain mingled with the salt spray which rose like columns of white smoke from the sea. The wind was so strong that she dared not raise her head for fear that if she did it would precipitate her on the bare rocks below.

She could run no longer. She fell down by a stone and hid her face on its cold surface. Above her head a fig tree flapped its leafless branches. The lightning circled round the sky; but she saw it no longer. She could only see the thing from which she had fled, and which seared her brain, cleaving it, as it were, into two. She saw it now, when her face was pressed against a stone and her eyes closed. Were she to open them she would still see a woman in a dark skirt and crumpled white blouse, broad-shouldered, with a heavy coil of dark hair on the nape of her neck and hands clasped together; a woman walking slowly, so slowly that one could count her footsteps towards a door; slipping behind it, dumb as a spirit. The awful slowness of her movements; the slowness of her shadow creeping up the wall and across the ceiling, as though returning to the last ray of sunlight which gave it birth. And the sound of laughter in that room; high, thin laughter, like the quavering echo of a sob.

Wrestling with that vision, she beat the ground with her hands. Her teeth closed on the flesh of her own arm. Better to have one's eyes burnt out by the lightning than be defeated by a living ghost; better be tossed by the gale into the sea than count those footsteps across the yellow floor. Again the door closed. Again that demoniacal laughter sounded above the storm.

She lay there even when the thunder had retreated far away and the lightning played fitfully across the green line of sky on the horizon. The rain fell in slow, warm drops; the trees, which had been bent to the ground, straightened out their quivering branches; a troop of migrating birds rose into the sky from its hiding-place among the rocks. The storm had passed, and when a pale sun set in the wind-driven clouds it left a long trail of yellow light across the sea.

X

A FEW DAYS AFTER the storm, which broke the spell of fine weather, Abramovitch received a letter from Maria Ivanovna asking him to go and see her. He went immediately.

The maid said that 'the signora' had been ill, but was now a little better. Perhaps he had come to advise her about her health. He nodded and went into the sitting-room. There was nothing unusual in the way she sat by the window; but even before she turned her head towards him he realised that something had happened.

'She knows,' he thought, carefully making his way between a chair and a small table on which stood a yellow glass jar.

'How are you? The maid told me you had been ill.'

She ignored his question.

'Vera Bernini has been to see me,' she said, and he felt that she was watching his face. He did not reply at once. He understood now what had puzzled him during the last days. Vera had not been herself since that terrible storm, which she said had overtaken her in the street. She was silent and absentminded. One afternoon, when he had come on her unawares, he had seen a look he could not forget in her eyes. It was the look of someone afraid of her own thoughts. Perhaps she understood that she had given herself away, because she turned on him with fury.

'How dare you come creeping in like this? Your boots squeak. I thought it was a chair,' she had said. Involuntarily he had compared her then to an animal wounded to death and hiding its pain. Now he knew whence that pain had come.

He could find nothing to say. With deep pity he looked into her face and waited for her to speak. At last she said:

'You know why she came. I wanted to tell you what I am going to do. I must go to England and get a divorce.'

'Yes,' he replied. 'Homoutov is leaving for England in a few days' time. Perhaps you could travel together. It would be easier for you.'

She assented, and a moment later, after discussing the details of her journey, he rose to go. Although she seemed so calm he was afraid of leaving her alone.

'You don't mind being by yourself like this?' he asked.

'No, I am accustomed to it.' She tried to smile. He remembered how she had smiled at him standing in the rain on the doorstep of the house, and his heart contracted with pity for her.

'I wish I could have spared you this,' he said, taking her hand.

'It had to come. Besides, I think I really knew before.' She turned her face away so that he should not see her trembling lips, and without saying another word he went out.

During the days that followed he could think only of her.

He was haunted by the memory of her face, the quiet, list-less way in which she spoke, the self-control he noticed in her least gesture.

'It would be better,' he thought, 'if she did not survive it. But she will live for years, bound to that awful suffering. She will never get over it. He has killed that power in her.'

He had no difficulty in persuading Homoutov to accompany her to London. His conscience, he assured Abram-ovitch, was never easy. If only he had known! He would have done everything in the world to prevent such a catastrophe. Now that it was too late he would do what he could to help her. He would take care of her in London – it was difficult alone for a foreigner.

On the morning of her departure Abramovitch rose early, and with special care brushed his shabby clothes and old battered hat, to which sun and rain had given a peculiar green colour. He was known by it. If any of his acquaintances caught sight of his figure in the street he never failed to say:

'There's Abramovitch. One can't miss him because of that impossible hat.'

This morning as he passed a brush over its surface, which somewhat resembled a faded map of the world, so many contours and figures had the rain drawn upon it, he did not stop to wonder why he was taking special trouble with his appearance. He did so rarely; but today it was with the half-conscious feeling that he must in every way show his regard and affection for her whom he would see for the last time.

He left the Villa without disturbing anyone. A thin grey

mist clung to the trees and hid the house from his view even before he had reached the gate. It was cold and damp. He shivered as he was rowed out to the boat in his *dghaisa*. Maria Ivanovna was on deck among a crowd of passengers. He saw her at once because there was something about her figure which distinguished her from other women. In his mind it was associated with the beauty of Madame Leonidov before she had taken to wearing high collars, and become conscious of the fascination of her voice. She was waiting alone for him. Homoutov had disappeared, dragged away, as she explained, by an old friend with whom he was exchanging reminiscences.

On his way to the harbour he had turned over in his mind what he would say to her. It was his last chance to express that of which she had convinced him. He did not often feel the desire to express his convictions. Most people he knew killed that desire in him; but with Maria Ivanovna he felt the need of speech – not for that which one was obliged to say, but that which one thought and left unsaid.

He had brought a few flowers – white roses, no longer fresh, but lavishly sprinkled with drops of water which looked like dew. He gave them to her, and fixing his eyes on the narrow brim of her hat, from under which stray wisps of hair escaped, curling round her forehead, he said:

'I hope you will think of me sometimes. Forgive me for my clumsy words, but I want to tell you that I think you are a brave woman. Courage, my dear, is the essential virtue. However good you are, you can never be free without it; and it is the desire for freedom which you must always keep alive in you. I cannot explain, but perhaps you will understand what I mean. It is only cowardice which makes men fools and slaves to their own selves. Never forego your freedom. Struggle for it all your life. I know you can – one of the very few . . .'

He stopped, afraid that she might be offended by his words. But she seemed to understand him, although he had spoken at random, scarcely knowing what he said. She took the roses and assured him that, whatever happened, she would try to find what he called her 'freedom'.

'I will always remember that,' she said. A thorn pricked her ungloved hand, and, twisting a handkerchief round her bleeding finger, she smiled. He noticed everything she did, the least, the most insignificant of her gestures, as though trying to imprint the image of her person unforgettably on his mind.

A faint mist hovered over the water like smoke slowly drifting down the wind. The outlines of the ships were blurred by it. Valetta seemed distant and unreal. The people walking about the deck seemed unnaturally large until they approached, and, as the mist retreated from them, suddenly shrank to their normal size.

The intangible melancholy of autumn seemed alive in this greyness. It gripped the heart, making it ache with a restless, unhappy longing for the indefinable and unknown.

When the bell clanged Abramovitch began to hurry, afraid of being left behind. He ran towards the companion ladder, then remembering that he had not seen Homoutov, ran back again; but it was too late, and he was hustled along with a crowd of people. He left her leaning over the side of the rail, the white roses in her hand. She waved to him and he strained to see her as long as he could; but directly he reached the quay he went away without once looking for the white funnels of her steamer.

Instead of returning to the Villa he wandered about the streets, agitated by an emotion which made him so far forget himself that he passed Kondratieff without recognising him, and did not raise his hat to the Dowager Countess, who drove by in a *carrozin*, with a yapping dog and a maid, who found it hard to cling to the shining, slippery seat.

For Maria Ivanovna had awakened a desire which he had stifled for years. The way he thought and acted was always as clear to him as the way that others thought and acted. He found it easy to analyse his own moods without giving way to self-deception, but he could not understand why in the presence of this woman his mind had reverted to longings which he had long since thought dead. There was that in her which forbade pity and inspired confidence.

'Is it possible,' he thought, 'that she will free herself from shame and misery; that she will not allow herself to be dragged down by it? A brave spirit, yes, a brave spirit.' He repeated the words many times, because they seemed to allay his doubts about himself. Something urged him to follow the example she had set. Had he not spoken to her of freedom, of the independence of soul that he had valued so highly and nevertheless lost? Perhaps it was not too late to go back now; perhaps he could still live a few quiet years, free from the love which had shackled him so long. If only he could keep the memory of her in his mind, and not allow his weakness to obliterate it . . .

Someone touched his arm. He looked up to see the

massive figure of Bassanov. His dislike of the great man forced his head farther into his shoulders, and he said in a glum voice:

'Ah, how are you? Very glad to meet you.'

Bassanov gazed at him with his narrow somnolent eyes, and raising his upper lip in an ironical smile said:

'My good friend, do you know that I have just come from the Villa, and that they have been waiting for you since the morning? Madame Leonidov is quite upset. She thinks you forgot to come off the boat. Beauty in distress, you know.' He closed one eye and with the other surveyed Abramovitch's sullen countenance. Then realising that he was only wasting his wit on a dull fool, he gave him another look with both eyes, and walked on whistling 'La Donna e Mobile' through his teeth.

Abramovitch went back to the Villa. Madame Leonidov was alone in the drawing-room, and sitting among all her things – the yellow-faced miniatures, the unframed ancestor over the mantelpiece, the many knick-knacks scattered everywhere – she reminded him of some forgotten goddess enshrined with her treasures around her.

This winter, he reflected, the house would be lonely; there would not be many visitors. He knew that Madame Leonidov's influence was declining. Her imperious ways were resented. Somebody – he thought it was Vera – had started the rumour that her father had been a village schoolmaster who had had an affair with the local nobleman's daughter; and the Dowager Countess told everyone that she had always known that Madame Leonidov was not of the aristocracy.

As, when he came in, she turned her clear shining eyes

172

on him, he was yet again struck with wonder at the beauty of her face. She was idle for once, and even her cards lay untouched on the table beside her.

'Well, has she gone?' she said.

'Yes. I went on board. There were not many people going.' He paused to see if she would make another remark, but, as she did not, he went on: 'I met Bassanov in Valetta. He said you were waiting for me. Do you want anything?'

'No. I am prepared to be always the last person considered by you.'

She spoke resentfully, but he was too full of his own thoughts to notice that she was upset. He turned his back to the light so that she would not be able to see his face, and without looking at her said:

'Elena Michailovna, I too want to go.'

'What do you mean?' Her voice rose. 'Go? Where? Why?'

'Oh, it does not matter – anywhere. But I am tired of this life we have been leading here so long.'

She understood him now, and understood what had forced him into this admission.

'Who is keeping you? It would lessen my expenses, you know.'

He winced. But it was too late to retreat, and rattling the stones in his pockets to give himself confidence he replied:

'It had to come to this some day, and you know it as well as I do. I have given you everything. Why should you grudge me a few years, a little time to get back something of what I have lost? You do not love me. I doubt if you ever have, but you have succeeded in making me what I am – the necessary appendage of a beautiful woman. Perhaps it is not really your fault. Your beauty has ruined me. It has sapped my strength and made me old before I had realised that I was no longer young. For years I have been the butt of your scorn and of the mockery of your friends – I admit I deserved it. It has been my reward for following you everywhere like a dog, for obeying you as no man should obey a woman who doesn't love him. I am a fool and you despise me rightly for my folly. But now that you have no use for me you must let me go.'

Calm and placid, she moved a little so that the light fell on her gleaming hair and the back of her neck, but left her face in shadow.

'And what is to become of me?' she said, keeping her voice as low and toneless as she could. 'Have you thought of that, my friend? You will start your life again, and I shall remain here to watch my ugly daughter grow up into a caricature of what I once was! Of course, I never expected anything else. I knew that when I grew old, worn out by my cares for you and all the stupid people who are for ever expecting to have my money and my favours, you would want to leave me. Your selfishness has been like a chain round my neck ever since Leonidov died.'

Carried away by her words, she was losing her attitude of calm indifference. A shrill note of anger crept into her voice.

'But I know that all men are like that, selfish, cruel, heartless. You are worse than the rest because you pretend to be so meek. There was no need for Charles Wilson to show you how to leave a woman. Oh, I know what you are after! You can't deceive me by talking about your freedom and your new life. You think you have the right to go. Go, then; but when she has left you don't come back and ask me for pity.'

'How dare you talk like that!' he shouted, trying to drown her words by his. 'You are mad!'

His loss of self-control calmed her.

'No,' she answered more quietly, 'but I know one thing – you cannot cut yourself off from me because there are too many years behind us. It is time that counts.'

'It cannot when there is nothing to bind us together. I only beg you to set me free of your own will because . . .'

She interrupted him.

'What? A beautiful action? – *Madame Leonidov congédiant son amant*? Most resourceful of you to suggest it – and convenient, I dare say – but if you are not too old to begin your life again, I am too old for this attitude of the *tragédienne*. You honour me, but I must decline to hold the stage to the applause of all our friends.'

She had risen and was striding about the room pushing the chairs which stood in her way. Abramovitch said nothing. He was aware that he risked defeat in listening to her, but he was robbed of all capacity for action by a sense of futility which was like the inertia of despair. He could only stand and watch her rave.

Then Madame Leonidov, guessing perhaps that her fury would only serve to increase his obstinacy, changed her mode of attack. She came close up to him and gazed earnestly into his face, her eyes filled with tears, which only made them seem more beautiful.

'You loved me once,' she said. 'Have you forgotten? Do you wish to take from me what you gave? Forgive my hasty words, my anger; but you do not understand how bitter it is for a woman to realise that she is too old to be loved; to know that only the young are beautiful.'

Her voice softened; she evidently enjoyed saying these words.

'I am alone. I am weak,' she continued, and the tears which had trembled on her eyelashes rolled down her cheeks. 'I need your support, your . . .' she hesitated . . . 'your kindness. Perhaps I have spoilt your life, but it is too late to alter the past. Here in exile you cannot forget it alone. Let me help you.' She checked an impulse to say, 'At least I have money,' and changed it to 'At least you can have what my poor love is worth.' She held out her hand. With a great effort of will she had regained a semblance of her usual composure. She turned her face a little to one side, so that he should not see the marks that the tears had made on it.

He knew that if he gave way now it would be forever. The hope, the new and vital impulse, which unknowingly Maria Ivanovna had stirred in him, would vanish if the image of her person faded from his mind. He could not give up his desire for freedom to be dragged back to the old lies and self-deceit. He saw her leaning over the rail, her pale, tired face above the heavy-headed white roses, smiling to him as though calling to him to follow. 'A brave spirit,' he had said this morning. 'Courage is the essential virtue.' He raised Madame Leonidov's hand to his lips.

'Goodbye,' he said.

'No, not goodbye. I cannot let you go. Why not a new life – with me?'

Her beautiful voice was tender. He felt her other hand on

his head, drawing him towards her, forcing oblivion on his rebellious mind. Suddenly he felt tired, too tired to resist; and he knelt down before her. He had loved her too much once to leave her now. He could rebel no longer; he could strive no longer against his own weakness. It was too late. His weary mind patiently hammered out these thoughts; but his heart ached at the bitter, unwished-for surrender of his last hopes.

Stroking his thin grey hair, Madame Leonidov smiled at her triumph. She had never yet failed to revive his devotion for her. It was impossible that she should fail. She knew his moods, his restless cravings too well; but her power did not blind her to the fact that this time the odds had been heavy against her. His dejection told her more eloquently than words how nearly she had lost. And it was all through Maria Ivanovna, whose youth had been a torment to her, whom she had always feared as a rival. She felt that today she had striven against her hateful spirit – defeated in the end, of course, but at a great risk. She could not count on many more victories. Her position among the Russians was no longer secure; it had been slowly undermined; and she knew that if Abramovitch left her now she would be deserted by everyone.

This afternoon she had been upset because that wretched, conceited Bassanov, who owed everything to her, had refused to play because he said the piano was not good enough. A short while ago he would not have dared. It had been as a first warning of the loss of her power. And now she no longer felt the strength to fight intrigue and counter the assaults of mischief-makers.

She was tired. This struggle with the man whom she needed as a buffer between herself and the world had exhausted her. She would never dare risk another defeat. These scenes were bad for her. She must take care of herself. Whatever happened, she must not lose her beauty – the last, the unfailing weapon.

It was cold; the rain had begun to fall. She felt a draught on her back; it was bad for her. She must shut that window – it was too damp now to have the windows open in the evening.

PART TWO

I

NO. 129, BARDOLF ROAD, a grey, square, five-storeyed building, was distinguishable from the uniform row of houses on either side of it only by one feature which, at first sight, almost negligible, assumed a special importance in the eyes of those who understood its significance. It was the large brass plate which was affixed, not to the door, but to one of the flat stone pillars which flanked the steps leading up to it. There it could he seen by everybody, and there every passer-by could read its laconic message to the world:

Doctor James,
Physician and Surgeon.
Daily from 2–5. Saturdays, 10–1.

Although this brass plate and the words it bore were not in the least original or capable of provoking curiosity, every-one who knew the house interpreted them in a different way. The doctor's wife believed that it had an intimidating influence on beggars and errand boys, and the notice, 'No hawkers; no circulars,' had not been affixed to that part of the iron railings which belonged exclusively to No. 129.

'We have never had to put it up, you know,' she would say; 'there's been no trouble with them at all. It's being in the profession and letting them know it that keeps them away, I believe.'

The neighbours, on the other hand, surveyed the brass plate with a scepticism not to be dispelled by Mrs James's circumspect remarks about her husband's profession. What was the use of having it there when no one ever saw a patient enter or leave the house?

It was as clear to Mrs Green in No. 127 as it was to the solicitor's family opposite in No. 128, that whereas Dr James never received a patient, Mrs James received paying guests. In other words, No. 129 was a boarding house, invaded by the same smells, regulated by the same laws, providing homely comfort for the same sort of people as every other boarding house in Bardolf Road. Behind the green door with its knocker in the shape of a clenched hand, were concealed the attributes essential to such an establishment: linoleum-covered floors, palms to fill and decorate every corner, unceasing sounds of acrimony in the dark and unexplored regions of the basement.

The brass plate served only as a sign of the past, which according to some had never existed. It created a delusion, which, notwithstanding the outspoken comments of the neighbours, who resented its presence as though it were a personal offence, was carefully maintained by the solicitude of Mrs James like some hallowed tradition, on which rested the dignity of her house. It was handed down through the hierarchy of visitors, who succeeded one another with unfailing regularity, according as the winter dwindled into a spring heralded by the first bank holiday, or a summer marked by the advent of foreigners and sight-seers took its place. All these people whom Mrs James knew as the 'permanents' of the winter months, or the 'weekenders' of the summer, took it for granted that the Doctor was a busy man. In that profession, of course, one had not very much spare time. Sometimes he spent whole afternoons in that little study, with the roll-top desk. Very hard-working indeed he was.

It would have been indiscreet to inquire what Doctor James always did when he was left alone in the company of his desk, but somebody had once volunteered the information that he drank. Of course the rumour had been suppressed. Such a charming, affable man as the doctor! It was preposterous! One might as well accuse Mr Jacobe himself of these excesses. To those who knew him, the bare idea of Mr Jacobe's (and therefore the doctor's) insobriety was absurd, for Mr Jacobe was the pillar of the boarding-house. He counted for more than the brass plate; he even counted for more than the doctor himself. Without him and his wife, No. 129 (it was always known as that – Mrs James had wanted to call it 'The Laurels', because it overlooked some gardens from the back, but the doctor had insisted that a professional man's house should have no name) could never have attained solid respectability. He and his wife helped to make it a success, and they were very privileged. They had been there long enough to he considered not only as 'permanent' but fixed for ever. They sat at a small table in the dining-room, they had butter at meals, and in the evenings Mrs Jacobe wore a dress with a lace front. As far as it was revealed to outsiders, everyone knew the habits of their private life. No one who ever estimated the importance of that pat of butter on their table forgot to take into consideration the rival fact that they never took a bus. For it was known that Mr and Mrs Jacobe always walked. They could be seen walking down Oxford Street, past Marble Arch, and through Kensington Gardens every morning of their lives. They could be seen walking in other parts of London at other times of the day. They had been seen in the City, and they had been seen at Kew. It was consequently enough for Mr Jacobe to open his mouth and allow the words 'My wife and I' to escape from thin, discreetly pursed lips, for anyone listening to see Mr and Mrs Jacobe walking side by side down Oxford Street. The typist, whose bobbed hair was too long, and whose life was governed by the fear of catching cold, so that she always smelt of eucalyptus, declared that she often saw Mr Jacobe, and Mrs Jacobe of course, walking into a block of offices in Cheapside. But no one was quite prepared to believe her, because it was known that she had a habit of giving information based only on her desire to have notice taken of her. Besides, the privileged Mr Jacobe of the boarding house dwindled into the very insignificant wearer of a bowler hat in the street. It would be quite easy to mistake him! So that, in spite of the efforts of all the boarders, and especially of the eager, inquisitive lady, whose husband was a film actor abroad and who had once endeavoured to tempt Mrs James out of her discretion, the mystery, if such a word indeed was applicable to people as respectable and worthy as the

Jacobes, remained unsolved. No one could surmount the barrier of Mr Jacobe's impassive 'My wife and I' . . .

This year the boarding house had settled down earlier than usual to the monotony of the winter months. The 'permanents' had all of them appeared in September. Mrs James considered herself very lucky. She was 'full up' except for one small room at the top of the house.

'So nice to think we're fixed up for the winter!' She beamed on the 'permanents', who always resented intruders.

Nevertheless it was she herself who one day at lunch announced the startling news that the boarding house was to welcome another guest. Being a timid woman, to whom life had for forty-six years taught the lesson that 'it wasn't any use taking on, because everybody had a kink somewhere,' she chose the moment when carving the joint, with her back to the room, to announce the arrival of a stranger.

'She is staying quite a long time, I believe,' she said, as with a dexterous movement she flicked a bit of meat off the point of the knife on to a plate. 'A married lady and a foreigner. Going to be in London several months.' The atmosphere was charged with the familiar smell of steam, cabbage and moth-eaten stuffs. The boarders assembled round the long table had inhaled it for several minutes. Their resentful minds ruminated upon the fact that Mrs James was being very slow with the mutton and that she had no business to surprise them with disagreeable news at such an inopportune moment. It was an unwritten rule of the boarding house that there was no conversation before the sweet. And Mr and Mrs Jacobe had been served of course. They never had to wait.

Mrs Jacobe, the first to be satisfied with mutton, was the first to express her discontent. She was a woman with a yellow complexion, red hair dressed in such a way as to suggest that it was not all her own, and a habit of making none but strictly necessary and pointed remarks. People said that her husband was afraid of her, but of course they were a devoted couple.

'And the husband, Mrs James?' she inquired from her end of the room.

'Oh, I don't know anything about him,' replied Mrs James, and subsided uneasily into her chair. The doctor raised his heavy jaw from his plate. His handsome, sallow, chinny face always wore a sullen, angry look. He never allowed his features to relax into a smile, as though all his energy was spent in keeping people in awe of himself.

'Come, come, Mrs Jacobe,' he said, raising his eyebrows so as to indicate that he was in a mood for banter. 'Isn't this a little indiscreet?'

'Oh, doctor, what a naughty man you are!' She wagged a thin, pointed finger in front of her nose. 'You know, I didn't mean anything.'

At that moment the door opened, and someone, at first concealed by the leather screen round the door, came into the room. Everyone immediately became aware of the fact that an extra place had been laid at the table, and the murmur of conversation provoked by the interval after the mutton subsided abruptly. Mrs James bustled out of her chair.

'This is Mrs Wilson,' she said, as the newcomer appeared round the screen. Obeying a common impulse, everyone looked up with a hostile stare. An intrusion in the middle of lunch was unprecedented. Clearly it pointed to something unusual in the character of the intruder.

'This is your place at the bottom of the table, I think' – Mrs James hovered about like an anxious hen – 'next to Mr Jones.' The woman sat down. Mr Jones, a chinless youth, who hailed from 'way down Connecticut', moved his chair to make more room for his neighbour, and, having loudly cleared his throat, passed her the salt. Then, satisfied that he had done his duty, he returned to his occupation of rolling bread pellets. The rest of the meal passed in silence. Stewed prunes were difficult things to handle, when there was a newcomer to examine. She seemed uneasy, like one who is not accustomed to eat in close proximity to strangers. Otherwise she was ordinary enough. The typist and her friend decided that she was not interesting. The commercial traveller, whose face was the colour of sun-warmed brick, thought that 'she mightn't be bad to talk to – a quiet little thing.' The film actor's eager and inquisitive wife fixed her attention on the lady's wedding ring, which she wore on her right hand. The last member of the party (except for the Jacobes, who of course showed no curiosity) could not take his eyes off her. He was the only foreigner who had hitherto penetrated within the exclusive, respectable walls of No. 129, and he had been there so long that in the eyes of the boarders he was almost exonerated from the blame of not being English by birth. Although he was a Pole and his name was Panzadski, he was privileged. He could even joke with Mr Jacobe about the days just after the war when during the peace celebrations Mr Jacobe had lost five shillings. Pickpockets were really very skilful!

He was neat and dapper, with a flat little moustache and a roving eye. He never made himself conspicuous, but he knew it was on him that the boarding house depended for entertainment. It was generally conceded that Mr Panzadski was 'always full of anecdotes'. Besides his mirth-provoking powers, this gentleman had an eye for women. Mrs James, who had a fondness for the expression, might have said had she suspected any such quality in him that he 'had a way with them'. He himself was fully aware of the fact that few could resist his rather charming smile and soft insinuating voice. Directly Mrs Wilson appeared he gave his moustache a reflective twirl and set himself to examine her at leisure. Chance did not often vouchsafe him the opportunity of gazing at a woman with beautiful eyes and hands which he mentally described as 'tender'. Yes, that was the right word. He already relished the thought of kissing them as a preliminary to something better. When he had reached this stage in his reflections Mrs Wilson must have become conscious of his stare, because she raised her eyes and looked at him. Unfortunately her glance did not stop at his face, but travelled from it to the mantelpiece decorated with artificial flowers, then towards the window, where it met the furtive glance of Mrs Jacobe's green eyes, and from which it sought refuge in watching Mr Jones's red fingers feverishly rolling bread pellets. When at last the meal ended and the commercial traveller pushed back his plate with a loud yawn (he was not at all well-mannered; Mrs Jacobe had frequent cause to deplore his lack of refinement), the company proceeded one by one into the drawing-room, sweeping the reluctant newcomer along with them. Although she had already been in that room, it still gave her a slight shock of surprise, because it bore such eloquent witness to the efforts of Mrs James, and her mother before her, to preserve anything that they had ever possessed. There were in it a great many plush-covered chairs with twisted legs and high, uncomfortable backs. There was a hard, narrow sofa, flanked by a glass case full of little cups and china shepherdesses, attached to curly-headed, sheep-like dogs. There were bunches of pampas-grass in the corners and oil paintings of still life in heavy, gilt frames on the walls. There were palms which had a dry, withered look, on high stools in front of the lace-curtained windows. On the top of the piano, protected by a green baize runner, stood photographs of family groups. The industry of many generations had placed antimacassars on the back of every chair. In that room there was the peculiar smell which lingers round old furniture, and to Mrs Wilson it seemed that it clung not only to the walls but to the people who year after year sat in a narrow semi-circle, looking at the embroidered fire-screen which represented a bird of paradise in a wreath of flowers. Her heart contracted with the pain which the homeless readily feel in unfamiliar surroundings. She shrank from this little self-contained universe into which she had stepped as if by mistake.

Meanwhile the *habitués* had taken up their customary places: Mrs Jacobe on the sofa, Mr Jacobe under the palms, the actor's wife on the piano stool, which was too high for her short, pink silk legs, and Mr Panzadski on the low chair by the fire-place. The others scattered over the remaining furniture. Mrs Wilson found herself beside Mrs Jacobe. It seemed to her that there was a cautious, deferential look about these people, as though they were occupied in preventing any infringement on their privacy by forced politeness and jocularity. Alone the Jacobes were secure from the onslaughts of the unwary and the curious.

It was therefore Mrs Jacobe who made the first attempt to draw the lady on her left into conversation. Fixing her eyes on Mrs Wilson's chin, she said:

'I am Mrs Jacobe. That is my husband.'

Without opening his mouth, Mr Jacobe made certain sounds, which freed him from the obligation of speech, and pressed his chin a little more firmly on his collar. The bald crown of his head encircled with thin, reddish hairs shone in the light which fell on it from the window. His face, with its long aquiline nose, had the look of a bird of prey startled out of frowning placidity. No amount of security could dispel that look. It was frozen on his features like a grimace on a child's face when its attention has for a moment been distracted from the business of crying.

'We hear you are going to be here quite a long time,' continued Mrs Jacobe in her rasping voice, which sounded as if it were arrested half-way in her long, bony throat. 'You don't know London, I suppose?'

'I was here a great many years ago.'

'Well, well, not quite a stranger, I see,' put in the commercial traveller with a laugh meant to sound encouraging. Mrs Jacobe took no notice of him. She wanted information, and she hated being interrupted when she was bent on acquiring it.

'If you will excuse a personal remark, you speak English very well for a foreigner.'

'My husband is English.'

'Quite, quite. Wilson, I believe, is a typically English name.'

There the conversation seemed bound to stop, but Mrs Jacobe was a woman of determination. She wasn't to be put off.

'You have had a long journey to England, I presume?'

'About four days.'

Mrs Jacobe asked herself whether the woman was shy or stubborn by nature. Turning her attention from Mrs Wilson's chin to the paste buckles on her own shoes, she remarked tentatively:

'I went to Italy once. On my honeymoon.'

Mr Jacobe stirred under the palms.

'My wife and I,' he said, pressing his finger-tips together, 'thought it a beautiful country. So warm,' he added, as if to explain the beauty he mentioned.

'Yes, they have no fogs there,' said the typist, who always complained of the cold and always sat nearest the fire.

'Ah, fogs, no!' Mrs Jacobe allowed a sigh to escape her firmly encased lungs.

'I suppose you lived in the South?' She gave the obstinate chin another look.

'Yes.'

Really it was unheard of! That she should be driven to ask 'where?' as if she had been that inquisitive woman whose actor-husband was only an excuse! The answer was 'Malta.'

'How delightful!' chorused everybody with the forced animation which with them was a sign of curiosity struggling against boredom.

'They've a kind of fever there,' said Mr Jones, emerging from behind his *Daily Mail* and yet again reminding Mrs

Jacobe that he came from 'way down Connecticut'.

'They say that the internal organs . . .'

'Oh, Mr Jones,' exclaimed the typist and the typist's friend. Mrs Jacobe's sensitive nostrils twitched. She had always thought that Connecticut wasn't quite . . .

'Well, haven't I said that I was scientifically minded, if you see what I mean. It's nothing to sniff about, either,' retorted Mr Jones in an injured voice and, surprised at his own eloquence, dived behind the paper. His left hand made convulsive movements on his knee, as if it were in a great hurry to roll a great many pellets of bread.

'You have come to join your husband, I take it,' continued Mrs Jacobe, relentlessly pursuing her own train of thought.

'My husband is not in London.' The voice in which the words were spoken caused Mrs Jacobe to shift her gaze from the chin of the speaker to her eyes. Their steady glance defied her scrutiny, so that she was obliged to turn her head and say something about the weather – a conversational subterfuge which she employed rarely, and which invariably caused her husband to make some remark, prefaced by the words with which he reassured himself as with a slogan. This time he said:

'My wife and I feel the same about it. The English climate is most treacherous.' And Mrs Jacobe assented with a movement of the head calculated in no way to disturb her edifice of hair. She was beginning to feel a pleasant somnolence stealing over her. Presently she would doze. When she woke she would consider the significance of that Mrs Wilson's face when she was asked about her husband. Really,

Mrs James ought to be more careful about the people she took . . .

Mrs Wilson, seizing the opportunity of escape, went out, watched by several pairs of eyes. Mr Panzadski bestowed an appraising look at her full graceful figure, and his heart gave a pleasant flutter. If the lady's husband was not in London, what could be more propitious? He would not lose delay in making himself known to her. Besides, with a foreigner things were always so much easier! Judging from her dark hair and pale skin she might be Italian, or perhaps even a Pole, without any of that Israelite strain, which he for instance had inherited from his mother – a bright little Jewess from Cracow. With such thoughts in his mind, Mr Panzadski critically examined his long nails of which he was rather proud.

'A fine woman that,' remarked the commercial traveller, when the sound of Mrs Wilson's footsteps had died away. 'I bet she's got a good leg, or I am a Dutchman!' He was considered a little coarse, and liked to keep up the reputation. The girls giggled. Mr Jones blushed, but fortunately no one saw him do it. Mr Jacobe looked more startled and dignified than ever.

'My wife and I,' he began, but his wife was peacefully unconscious of the coarse man's lapse, and the censure died away unspoken on his lips.

Meanwhile Mrs Wilson had climbed the dark, slippery stairs, which grew narrower and darker with every floor, and was now sitting in her bare, ill-lighted room at the top of the house. It contained a chair and a small table by the window. An almanac had been stuck into the corner of the mirror, hung over the fireplace. Someone had attached a small wooden crucifix to the iron rail of the bedstead. It looked curiously out of place in that small, half-furnished room. The sense of its incongruity oppressed her, and she rose to take it away, but sat down again. It was not worth the trouble.

Her journey had effected little change in her, except that she felt the energy caused by reaction ebbing slowly away in the cold, stuffy atmosphere of London. It became increasingly difficult to fight against apathy, to keep herself from brooding over the same thing. She was quite alone now, because Homoutov's cheerful, loquacious presence had been withdrawn. Full of regrets and apologies, he had gone to Nottingham after installing her in a boarding house recommended by an English friend, and introducing her to the Russian authorities.

'They will do everything for you,' he had assured her at least twenty times in the last five minutes they had spent in each other's company at King's Cross.

'You must explain everything to them and leave it in their hands. I have known Zouboff, their secretary, for years. He is quite reliable and a most amusing man.'

He was genuinely distressed at being obliged to leave her.

'I wish I could put it off and stay to help you,' he said, pushing up his stiff little moustache so that his face took on a cocksure, rakish look, which went ill with his words. 'But the English never wait, you know. Business is business.' He repeated the words with evident satisfaction. He liked to think he was brisk and reliable and sure of himself like any English businessman.

He was light-hearted, and his sympathy for her expressed itself in his eager anxiety to be helpful, and in the imprecations he lavished on Charles Wilson's head. It solaced his conscience to call him a 'dirty English hound' under his breath and brandish his stick, as though it could slay all his foes for him.

Just before the train left the station she asked him if he knew Charles's address. He was very sorry, but he had forgotten it. It was some years ago that he had been to see him there, but of course he ought to remember. It was then that he had met – . He stopped, seeing a dull red rise slowly to her cheeks. Her embarrassment pained him the more that he had caused it by his own foolishness. Poor little woman! It was hard to be reminded of her misfortune like that. As the train jerked into movement he felt that with the thought of her suffering on his mind he would never regain his equanimity. It made one think. Since the war he had never had time or inclination for thought, but this business with Maria Ivanovna upset him. His own career had not been uneventful, but at least since his marriage he had been faithful to his wife in Madagascar. Life was simple enough if one didn't worry, but this could not bear reasoning about. It unbalanced him. He buried himself in the *Times* reports of companies' meetings, trying to forget.

She went back to the boarding house that he had found for her. Sitting in her room with her eyes on the dirty yellow walls, her mind travelled back to the Villa San Michele. They were very cultured and very refined there; they could distinguish so well between that which was vulgar and that which was licence according to gentility and *savoir-faire*.

They condemned gossip, but they admired wit. What could be more delightful than the gift of saying amusing things? Many of them possessed it. They enjoyed each other's sallies immensely. Madame Leonidov had at one time kept a little book in which she wrote down what the charming count had said about the long-necked Mademoiselle Strassoff, or what Vera repeated about the affair of Doctor Michailov and Madame P—.

There was, Maria told herself, little difference between them and these people among whom she was now. A little more polished in their ways, once a little more wealthy, and yet with the same anxiety to disguise their foibles by a multitude of conventions.

At one time she would have smiled at Mrs Jacobe as she had smiled at the beautiful Madame Leonidov, but lately her appreciation of the ridiculous and the mean had been sharpened into bitterness. She was convinced now that fear of each other and of themselves was the ruling power in their lives – a fear which had never penetrated her soul because it was excluded by the larger fuller vision which she had captured. Abramovitch would have called it 'freedom', but whatever it was it had set her above all bounded, vulgar interests and scruples, and she had clung to it with the passionate fidelity she brought to everything vital.

She had never been faced with moral conflict. Evil and the knowledge of human weakness had not left their mark on her. That was her mystery – the secret of her silence and her calm, the secret of the assurance which she involuntarily communicated to those who suffered from the tyranny of nerves. But now, almost accidentally as it seemed, her beauty had been marred and her happiness shattered. Someone had directed a blow at her which brought her down to the level of people like Vera and Madame Leonidov, like the boarders downstairs, people hedged in by fears and doubts, weak, bitter, perhaps unhappy, perhaps disillusioned, but always cowardly and furtive like mites living by mistake in the same big cheese.

She was tired of thinking. Her eyes travelled from the grey smudges of dirt on the walls to the window. A shadow lay aslant the sill. The sun must be shining. She would not mope indoors, but go out and pretend that she was like Homoutov, active and busy. She dabbed her aching eyes with water and, putting on her coat, went downstairs. As she crossed the narrow hall she heard the faint jingle of money, and a silver coin rolled up at her feet. It was half-a-crown. She stooped to pick it up and was wondering what to do with it, when an unfamiliar voice said close to her ear:

'Excuse me, Madam, but I think it is mine.'

She turned round and saw the young man who had stared at her during lunch. He smiled, showing even white teeth. His voice was soft. Everything about him seemed soft, from the hat he held to the silky little moustache which curled up at the corners of his wide mouth. She handed him the coin and was about to pass when he stepped into her way. Fortified by the knowledge (gleaned from the visitors' book) that she was Russian, he had hit on this little subterfuge to introduce himself.

'My name is Panzadski,' he said, and his brown eyes grew very soft. 'My nation is, I think, a near neighbour of

yours, and as you are a stranger here, perhaps an escort – ?'
He pronounced his 'r's'softly like a Russian.

'I know London quite well,' she replied without looking
at him again, and opened the door into the street. As she
passed him the faint smell of her clothes agreeably tickled
his nostrils. Close to, in the semi-darkness of the hall, she
had seemed more alluring even than at first. The swaying of
her hips as she walked tantalised him. He felt nettled. Was
she one of those haughty aristocrats he had learnt to hate in
his childhood? But never mind. A little patience and he
would get the better of her. Few women could resist his
insinuating ways. The thought of his charms consoled him
and he slid quietly into the drawing-room with a pleasant,
cheerful smile on his face.

Maria Ivanovna hurried down the street, afraid that he
might follow her. She had hoped to be left alone in this
respectable boarding house, but the inquisitiveness of Mrs
Jacobe and the advances of this gentleman with the caressing voice were ominous warnings. Alone, unprotected and
Russian, her position was intolerable. She could shield herself from their curiosity only by deliberate lies, and even
then for how long? With their watching eyes and plotting
brains they would in time discover her secret, and she
would find herself an outcast reviled by scandal-mongers,
driven from one house to another. She thought of Madame
Leonidov and Vera. They would never regret the way that
they had treated her. It was justified by the morality of
which they so frequently boasted. And everywhere it would
be the same. She would always be met with scorn and piti-
less righteousness.

She came to the hoardings opposite the Underground station, which was one of the advantages in Bardolf Road charged for by Mrs James, and, crossing the road, joined the stream of people who were disappearing down its passages. It was past four o'clock. This crowd, more leisured than the other which at six would pour out from behind counters and back offices, seemed to hurry from habit, or because it was anxious to disperse before it would have to wait for buses and jostle in trains. Maria Ivanovna, feeling that she too ought to be in a hurry, occupied with numberless cares, and above all anxious to get somewhere, took a ticket to Marble Arch. It did not matter to her where she went, so she repeated what the man in front of her said, and followed him into a crowded lift.

When she came out again into the street she stood a moment, wondering where she would go. Then, as her lonely figure had attracted the attention of a loafer standing near, she quickly turned her back on him and walked res-olutely towards the park. Although cold, the day was still and fine. White clouds, only here and there thickening into grey, hung in the sky, and the last rays of the sun gilded the topmost branches of the trees or stretched in long paths of light over the damp, short grass. The trees were bare, but the fallen leaves had not been swept away. They lay in thin, tidy lines along the low rails, which divided the lawns from the walks. Now and then the wind, which came in gusts round corners or swept across an open space, tore away a withered leaf, which still clung to its branch, and, having whirled it in the air, let it drop a lifeless thing upon the grass, to lie there looking like a crumpled piece of brown paper.

Those leaves, damp from the recent rain, and tidied away into thin heaps, stirred long-forgotten memories within her. She saw, as clearly as if she had stood there, a long avenue of elms bared by the first gales of autumn. It had been neglected; weeds grew on it, and the trailing stems of wild convolvulus clung, half-beaten down by the rain, to the first ridges of the tree-trunks. The rooks cawed overhead, flapping their heavy wings from branch to branch. The leaves had been tossed by the wind into crazy patterns over the ground or heaped into mounds, like drifts of snow after a storm. Through the decaying mass of brown here and there shone the gold of the birch or burned the red of the claw-shaped leaf of the maple. It was so pleasant to shuffle through these dead leaves and feel them cling like live things to one's feet and hear them rustle as if in answer to the wind. Their musty, acrid, lingering smell, which made the heart ache and sent it musing on cherished things, how well she remembered it! How faintly she could smell it now, rising like some thin ghost of the past from the edges of the swept, tidy walks.

She sat down on a seat and watched the sun sink behind a black ridge of roofs. It went down slowly, as if it could not pierce the grey sky, untinged by its flaming red. When at last it had disappeared, a thin, white mist rose from the water and streaked the clear, cold air. Forgetting that it was late, she sat there a long time. The people that passed all stared at her, and she was painfully conscious of their inquisitive looks.

'Why can't I be left alone?' she thought resentfully. Two girls talking in loud voices came up and sat down on the opposite end of the seat. They giggled a lot and threw long glances at her from under their tawdry hats. She noticed that the one nearest her had a large round hole in her stocking and that the naked flesh of her leg showed very pink against the dirty edge of torn silk. Her mind seemed to work independently of her will, registering facts which would probably have passed unnoticed by her if she had wanted to perceive them. She caught herself repeating the words:

'That girl's hands are blue with cold. If I took my gloves off, my hands would be blue, too.'

With a movement of impatience at herself, she turned her head, so as to distract her own attention, and watched a couple slinking hand in hand among the trees. She had again fallen into monotonous bewildering conjecture when the whispering of the girls on the seat startled her.

'Aw, come away. She mikes me gow all creepy loike, sittin' there in black loike a corse, never movin', and with that fice on 'er,' one of them said. The other one giggled. They both got up and walked away with many comments and much high piercing laughter. Their hasty retreat only made her feel more desolate. It hurt her that people should shrink from her as though there were something evil and ominous about her. She wanted to run after these girls and force them to come back and sit on the same seat with her. Bitterly she thought of Abramovitch's words. Free? How could she be free when she was so utterly beaten that the marks of her defeat were on her face to be seen by everyone! She was a prisoner to her grief and her anguish. There could be nothing beyond that for her.

Two figures, which seemed vaguely familiar, appeared round the corner of the path. They walked with determination and in complete silence, as though afraid that words would impede their progress. The man wore a bowler tilted over his nose. The woman walked bending forward from her hips. Who could they be? The man raised his bowler, the woman bowed and smiled. They passed her and presently vanished out of sight. Suddenly she remembered; the Jacobes, at the boarding house. The red-haired woman, who had tortured her with questions. Of course they *would* come upon her like this. Pursued, watched, haunted by inimical presences everywhere! Was there no escape? She hit the wooden seat with her hand. The pain she felt from it soothed her. She forgot the Jacobes, forgot the cold, and stayed there without moving, until the short November dusk merged into evening. She was the last of a small belated group of people to pass out of the gates by the Albert Memorial, and the keeper who watched her go grinned pleasantly at her, thankful that his day was nearly over. The chilly little crowd dispersed and she went back to Bardolf Road, which in the yellow gaslight of the street lamps seemed duller and gloomier than ever.

II

FEODOR SERGEIVITCH APOUHTIN, president of the Society for the assistance of emigrated Russians in England,
chairman of numerous committees and honorary secretary
of many others, reached the door of his house, in one of the
smaller streets of Belgravia, a quarter of an hour later on
this particular November morning than was his custom. He
returned regularly at ten minutes past one, having himself
witnessed the departure of all his officials for the luncheon
interval, but today it was twenty-five minutes past one
when he let himself in with his latch-key. As he divested
himself of his coat, the appetizing smell of cooking calf's
brains tickled his nostrils. That particular smell, which he
had vividly imagined on his walk from the nearest tube station, was very pleasant because it gratified both his hunger
and his love of stability. Having reached the age of fifty-five
with no greater vicissitudes than the loss of an official position (which he retained unofficially) and the gain of a rotun-
dity of figure, which was in no way detrimental to his
dignity, he allowed himself to become a man of habit. His
aversion for the unexpected included even the lesser things

of life. He liked to know beforehand what he was going to eat during the day. In the culinary almanac of the week Tuesday stood for grilled calf's brains at lunch, and he was pleased today, as he was pleased every day, to find the smell he had anticipated in the street faintly heralding his meal indoors. He mounted the carpeted stairs, feeling less unsettled and dissatisfied with the world because he had been detained an extra quarter of an hour. In the drawing-room his wife, his sister and a guest were waiting for him.

His wife was so small that not even the highest heels added anything to her stature. Her face, below her carefully waved black hair, was always contracted in a slight grimace which gave her, even when she laughed showing large uneven teeth, the expression of a peevish child. She wore long, curved nails, which made her thin hands look like claws. There was something Chinese, something a little dwarfish and uncanny beneath the smartness of her doll-like figure. In men sensitive to beauty, she excited faint repulsion – the involuntary nausea felt at the penetrating smell of the flowers of poisonous weeds. But she was an excellent and indispensable addition to the regularity of her husband's life. With her clothes, her admirable understanding of social duties, and the discretion which her ill-wishers said was entirely due to stupidity, she enhanced the dignity of his position. For twenty years he had been satisfied with her. Never had she given him any trouble as wives are apt to do, and she made up in elegance what she lacked in – well – beauty.

He paused at the door to survey the scene of his domestic happiness. He felt pleased with it. His wife had a piece of embroidery on her knee. His sister, with wisps of untidy grey hair framing her sharp-featured, quick-eyed face, seemed to add something intellectual and vigorous to the atmosphere. His guest Andreev, complacent and well-groomed, his full, clean-shaven face reflecting convivial goodwill, was enjoying one of his own anecdotes. His jovial, confident laughter rang through the room. Apouhtin decided that optimism was the only philosophy, and advanced towards them, his small, brown eyes gleaming behind his thick spectacles. Were it not for the spruce neatness of his clothes, he might well have resembled a fashionable, well-fed priest of the Orthodox Church, with his spectacles, his short grey beard and his fat, stubby-fingered hands. Familiarity precluded any greeting with Andreev, who only said, 'Ah, the president,' and continued his story, so he lowered himself into a chair, stretching his legs out in front of him as he felt the pleasant sensation of the lower portion of his spine in contact with something soft, yet firm. 'You are very late,' his wife remarked; 'I had to tell George to wait with lunch till half-past one.'

'Yes, I was kept at the last minute by a woman, who came to see me. A most unpleasant incident.'

He had not meant to remind himself of that incident before lunch, but now that he had started he might as well go on, although it *was* unpleasant. Very! 'She came to put her case to me and ask my advice. She lived in Malta – there are many Russians there, you know – and apparently met an Englishman, who married her and then went away to England. Having discovered that he was married already, she followed him.' He looked round with gravity.

'*Mais c'est tout à fait scandaleux*!' exclaimed his sister, who retained the habit, proper to what she considered Russian aristocratic circles, of speaking in French.

'My dear princess' (she was the widow of a Caucasian magnate), replied Andreev, a slight smile widening his well-curved mouth, 'Malta is known as a most profligate place. The navy! *Ces affaires là pullulent.*'

'Unfortunate woman,' said Madame Apouhtin, sticking her needle into the centre of a red silk flower.

'That is what I feel' – her husband flicked an imaginary grain of dust off his knee – 'the incident is most regrettable. I really don't know what can be done. As I pointed out to her, our position with the English is so extremely delicate that any scandal naturally tends to influence them against us. One cannot give way to prejudice. We have no rights and we ought to exercise discretion instead of behaving without any regard for the difficulties of the position in which we are so unfortunately placed.'

This was a favourite topic, and he could forget the pangs of hunger in the pleasure of hearing himself speak 'logically and without prejudice'. He derived great satisfaction in applying these words to his own arguments. Reasonable and without prejudice was what he prided himself on being, of unbiased mind and cool judgement, something of a philosopher and a critic of human nature as well as a hard-working, public-spirited official. These pleasant reflections, which flitted through his mind as he gazed at the top of Andreev's head, where the sleek, fair hair was carefully brushed over a thin spot, were interrupted by the white-gloved butler, who announced that lunch was ready. He was another indispensable feature of Apouhtin's household, second in importance only to his wife. Now that it was necessary to do without all luxury, he and his white gloves were a small compensation for the lesser miseries that Apouhtin endured.

At table the conversation flagged. Apouhtin discovered that his hunger overrode his anxiety, and it wasn't until the calf's brains had been superseded by another course that his wife said:

'Well, and what is this lady like? You have told us nothing about her. Is she young? pretty?'

Apouhtin always indulged feminine curiosity. It was not for him to censure the interests of the weaker sex. He leaned back in his chair, and with his thumb inserted the corner of his napkin into his waistcoat.

'I would not say she was pretty, but she has a certain charm. A healthy girl, by no means slim – a full figure, you know, although she is young, I should think. Quite a type,' he mused, his head a little on one side and his spectacles gleaming.

'Did you have any difficulty with her? Was she very upset?' asked Andreev.

'Oh, of course, but very controlled on the whole. She wants a divorce. We shall have to get her one, I suppose. It is a great bother, with all this difficulty about passports to China – you know, I was telling you the other day, but undoubtedly she must be helped. She does not know anyone, no parents, no relations. She broke down when she was telling me that she did not know that man's address. I did what I could. I comforted her. She seemed to go away a little cheered. Yes, I think I succeeded in comforting her. Her smile is most agreeable – a cultured woman! *bien élevée!*'

He gave the last word special emphasis, as though he had hit on a particularly appropriate and striking definition. Andreev smiled. He liked to think himself a humorist, and the idea of his friend comforting a woman with an agreeable smile pleased him the more that he knew many drawing-rooms where he could elaborate it to the advantage of his own reputation as a wit and a *raconteur*. Apouhtin seemed quite affected by the thought of himself in this new light of protector. At intervals during the rest of the meal he repeated several times, meditating as though to himself, 'Of course I consoled her. Moral support is the great thing. I reassured her and comforted her as well as I could.'

During the weeks that followed Maria Ivanovna learnt how slow and deliberate were the ways of Russian authorities. They were already in the first days of December, but so far her divorce was still under consideration. As often as she dared she went to Gordon Street, where the society had its new offices, and inquired whether they had found out her husband's address; the first step in the network of proceedings, which – as the president of it frequently assured her – would then follow. He was always amiable and never forgot to tell her that she was '*bien élevée*' and a woman whom no man should want to ill-treat, but nevertheless her feeling of distrust for him increased. There was something in the stare of his beady little eyes, shielded by very thick-lensed spectacles, something in his self-satisfied smile, that made her recoil from him. His urbane, effortless sympathy unnerved her, because she knew that it gave her no right to protest. Whenever she suggested that he should find her a lawyer, he replied:

'Maria Ivanovna, you must leave it to me. Our position is delicate, but I am doing my best to help you.'

If he had had an unsuccessful day, he varied the formula into: 'I must ask you to remember that we are all very busy. For instance, I have this question of passports to China on my hands.'

At last, wearied out by his excuses and evasive promises, she went herself to the offices of the P&O Company, in the hope that she would there learn something about her husband. She found her way into the Inquiries Department, and hesitatingly asked a clerk whether it was here that they could tell her the address of one of the company's officers.

'What ship was he on last?' he jerked at her across the counter. She did not know. He shrugged his shoulders and, closing a ledger with a snap that made the dust fly off its cover, he remarked that she had better write. But she could face no more unnecessary delays – besides, it was impossible to write. Clutching at a last hope, she asked if she could see a director. He saw that she was a foreigner and unworthy of his consideration.

'Oh, there are several of them,' he grinned, 'but they are not here, you know. Besides, they wouldn't see you in any case.' He hoped that she would go, and turned his back on her, but he could still see her out of the corner of his eye, standing in the helpless sort of way that women always did. Several times, when she thought that he was listening, he heard her say: 'It is essential that I should see somebody,' so at last, driven perhaps by his better nature, perhaps by the thought that he really had nothing better to do, he wandered over to speak to a girl seated at a typewriter. Maria Ivanovna heard nothing of their conversation, except that at the end the girl said: 'You'd better send her to Mr Smith.' He came back to the counter and asked her to wait. A moment later she was conducted by a small page-boy into a room at the end of a long corridor. As the door closed behind her a man dressed in tweeds of pepper and salt colour (he looked as if he was there only on his way to play golf) rose from his chair. He listened to her, fingering a paper knife on his desk.

'I understand you want the address of one of our officers,' he said, when she had finished speaking.

'Yes.'

'You realise, of course, that we are under no obligation to disclose it, even if we are able to identify the person you wish to trace.' He spoke in a quick, mechanical voice, as though he had learnt his words by heart, but it seemed to her that his shrewd, grey eyes looked kindly at her. Prompted by that look, she said, 'I am his wife, and I wish to bring an action for divorce against him, but it is impossible if I do not know . . .' she paused.

'Yes, I see. What name?'

'Wilson, Charles Wilson.'

The man smiled. 'I expect there are dozens of them. Can you give me any particulars?'

She told him what she could, and was startled as she spoke at the little she knew. He had told her nothing about himself, and what should she have asked? He had deceived her, and blindly she had allowed herself to be deceived. Resentment surged up within her at her own credulity. She had brought it on herself.

The following evening she received a thin, official envelope. It contained a lift of names. She read:

Captain C. Wilson. In command of *Ruritania*. Due to reach Bombay on December 30th, 1922.

Captain C. Tresham Wilson, on leave at 'The Shelter', Forham, Hants.

Charles R. Wilson, retired April, 1922, in consequence of ill-health. Formerly second officer on *Garrick*, B.I. line. Last address: 3, Michael Mansions, Bayswater.

Charles Wilson, on *Rowena*, bound for . . .

She read no more. Retired, ill-health, in April. It could be no one else. So he lived in Bayswater. Near enough for her to meet him in the street, with his wife perhaps. Oh, God, surely that was too much to bear! She must not think of it or she would go mad. She thrust the slip of paper into her pocket and left the house as she was, hatless and without a coat. As she ran to the nearest post office, the prayer rose to her lips, 'Oh, God, spare me from this. Have mercy on me – spare me . . .' The post office was closing, but she persuaded the man to send off her long telegram to Homoutov. He would be able to confirm the information she had obtained. He would be sure to remember the address.

She was right. The next day, with his telegram in her hands, she went to Gordon Street. The porter, who now knew her well by sight and also knew the reason of her visits (he and Apouhtin had had a chat about it only this morning, and His Excellency had remarked that the little lady was so anxious to get rid of her husband that perhaps there was another one concealed somewhere. Very jovial he'd been today. A man in a thousand was His Excellency), informed her, without moving from the chair in which he dozed all day, that the president was out and that Mr Zouboff, too, was out of town. She scribbled a few words with a stumpy pencil that he gave her and went away disheartened, because it seemed to her that she was farther than ever from her goal. Even now that she had the address would the president do anything for her? Probably she would not get her divorce before the spring. They had already wasted so much time. Why should she have to wait like this and eat her heart out month after month while Charles Wilson . . . No, she would not think of him. It made her feel faint and breathless, as if she were being strangled. She must keep her strength. She would need it afterwards, when she would have to find something to do.

As yet the thought of that 'afterwards' did not torture her. Now she was wholly obsessed by the fear that she would soon be penniless. She had very little money left, and when she had spoken of that to Apouhtin he had warned her that she must not count on the support of Russian organisations.

'It is my duty,' he had said, 'to remind you that our funds are very low, and that we have many responsibilities.

Especially at Christmas time it is impossible for us to provide for those who, like yourself, are placed in an unfortunate position.'

Besides, she was afraid that the boarding-house would learn her secret and that she would be turned out. She never imagined that it would be otherwise if they knew. They looked on her with suspicion, and it became more and more difficult to ward off their questions. She could not satisfy their curiosity, and she could not rid herself of the fear that they spied on her. Wherever she was – even in her cold, dark room at the top of the house – she felt their hostile eyes on her, penetrating, as it were, into the depths of her soul. She avoided them, but it was impossible to avoid long meals in the crowded dining-room and after-dinner conversations, when Mr Richards, the commercial traveller, was moved to heated eloquence about the state of the country, and what a shocking thing it was that the honest ratepayer should have to bear the burden of the chaos in Russia, while Mrs Jacobe, stern and upright on the sofa, silenced him with veiled remarks about the immorality of foreigners in general and Russians in particular.

Swamped in prejudice, the highest form of which was their narrow, destructive patriotism, they did not scruple to give vent to their scorn of what was foreign, and according to them – necessarily anti-British – foreigners (except, of course, that pleasant young man, Mr Panzadski) were objectionable, and above all not to be trusted. One heard of so many unpleasant things happening nowadays, after this war! Of course they none of them approved of scandal, and they were all ready to be nice, but was it not natural that this Mrs Wilson should be the centre of their gossip? She was the new thing about which they could exchange ideas, without ever bringing to light any of the secret foibles, which were treasured deep in the privacy of their own souls. Since her arrival, therefore, they had all been more intimate together and more of a 'family party', as her friend remarked to the typist when she knew she would not be overheard by Mrs Jacobe. Mrs Jacobe herself had relaxed sufficiently to take notice of the timid Mr Jones, who she discovered had quite a remarkable gift for acquiring information. Of course, no man, whose birthplace was Connecticut and who had such pernicious habits as rolling bread pellets, could be admitted into the circle of the privileged, which was imperceptibly ruled by that god of mirth Mr Panzadski, and consisted of the Jacobes, the doctor, his wife and his wife's mother, Mrs Horner, a woman of generous proportions, and with a disconcerting deafness which she assumed or discarded at will. But where before Mr Jones was allowed to blush unseen (which he did frequently, Mrs Jacobe being such a tyrant, and Mr Richards so coarse!) now the whole drawing-room would sit gasping 'really' and 'you don't say so,' when he chose to reveal what he knew of the 'mystery woman', as Mr Jacobe, who had a secret and inexhaustible love of the thriller, had once called her. For instance, it was he who had brought to their notice the fact that during all the time that she had been at No. 129 she had not received one single letter. (That meant, of course, that her husband didn't write to her, and husbands usually did, unless . . .?) It was he who knew of her frequent visits to the offices in Gordon Street, and he again who had seen her in Hyde Park in the company of an oldish man with a beard, spectacles, and that increase in waist measurement which prevents one from taking any but the shortest steps. (That was in the early days, when Apouhtin was sufficiently influenced by the 'agreeable smile' of the lady he comforted so well to make himself late for lunch by escorting her through the park!)

On the evening when Mr Jones – 'the sleuth', thus Mr Jacobe to himself – was able to announce the news that he had met Mrs Wilson, hatless and panting, in the Bardolf Road Post Office, his words were greeted with profound silence. 'She had not got a coat on, and she never saw me,' he said, pushing out his lower lip, as he always did when he wanted to feel important, 'although I took my hat off to her just by the Tube station.'

Mrs Horner, who had come to spend the day and was in the drawing-room, because Dr James had a bad cold and Mrs James was looking after him – (before she had appeared Mr Richards had expressed the opinion that the doctor was tight, and that this cold business wouldn't take a baby in, but he had been hushed down by the ladies) – Mrs Horner, particularly large and imposing against the background of red plush, was the first to recover from her astonishment.

'Well, I don't know what to make of it, I am sure,' she remarked, smoothing the countless stiff black tucks of silk on her large bosom.

'If she's got a husband, why does she live here by herself?' exclaimed the impetuous wife of the film-actor. Of course they had all thought of it before, but they didn't like to say so. She *would* put her foot in it! The two girls giggled, but Mrs Jacobe turned a disapproving glance at the offender, because grave suspicions were entertained about the actor himself, and it wasn't *her* place to talk.

'Ah well you never know in this world,' yawned the commercial traveller, stretching himself till his muscles creaked. 'She's a good-looking woman all the same, whatever you ladies have to say about her.'

'Looks is all you care about, Mr Richards,' said the typist, archly thrusting out a thin, silk-stockinged foot, but she got no answer, because she was so far from having any looks that he had once called her a mangy cat. At this point Mrs Jacobe felt that it was time to interpose. One couldn't allow that sort of talk about a woman, who was probably a sinner. (In her heart Mrs Jacobe was convinced that she was.)

'Good-looking or not,' she said in an acid voice, 'it is very awkward to have a person you can't be sure of about the house. I was told that the room upstairs would be kept for occasional visitors.' Although she did not look at her, the remark was addressed to Mrs Horner, whose money was known to have financed the boarding-house in its first days. Those who complained always did so in her presence, because it was thought that 'if she hasn't got a say in things, who has?'

'Yes, and didn't she look ill at dinner?' put in the typist's friend, who was a kindly creature, and even looked after Mr Jones's chilblains when they broke in the cold weather. No one answered her. They had all noticed Mrs Wilson's pallor and the fact that she had refused pudding, but it was an infringement on the rules of a respectable boarding-house to talk of such things in such cases. 'After all, there might be reasons,' as Mrs Jacobe put it to Mr Jacobe in the privacy of their own bedroom.

There was, however, one member of the boarding-house who did not share the common interest in Mrs Wilson, and that was Mr Panzadski. He let them talk and secretly nursed his own grievance. For the pleasant, the good-natured Mr Panzadski had for the first time in his life a grievance and a disappointment. The haughty Russian had rebuffed his advances, and he was at last forced to admit that she was invincible. His charming smile turned her into stone; the appealing look of his eyes found no glimmer of response in her face; the tricks of hand and foot he had practised with success for fifteen years served him not at all. No woman had ever resisted him, and yet this one, if he met her – quite casually, of course – in the passage, hurried by as if he had been contaminated. It was a blow to his pride, and his wounded vanity gave him no peace. The more she scorned him, the more he burned. What he had intended as a pleasant little flirtation seemed to be turning into the one-sided love affair he had always judiciously shunned. What more humiliating than to feel all the pangs of desire for a charmer who considered him as part of the furniture? It wasn't even as if she had the beauty – yielding and soft – that he particularly admired, but there was some-thing . . . and over that something Mr Panzadski could have wept tears of rage. Goaded by his disappointment, he com-forted himself into the thought that if she wouldn't look at him he would at least get his own back on her somehow. He would show the proud little lady that she couldn't treat him like dirt under her feet, as Russia had for so long treated Poland. This admixture of patriotism made of his longing to do her a bad turn a glorious revenge, not only of his own wrongs but of those of his country, and strengthened his resolve. His heart was soft, and he preferred to back his actions with a noble motive. Idealism was so much in harmony with his temperament! It so happened that chance favoured him with the discovery of the secret which had for so many weeks exercised the imagination of all the boarders. One afternoon when he was coming downstairs he heard a man's voice asking to see Mrs Wilson. He suddenly remembered something he had left behind, and quietly ascended the flight of stairs to his room, where he sat down, near enough to the door to hear the steps of those who passed it.

When Maria Ivanovna, hastily summoned by the maid, entered the drawing-room, she found that her visitor was Zouboff, the honorary secretary of the Society and Apouhtin's right hand. He stood leaning with an air of detachment against the mantelpiece. He was tall and, for his age, with a good figure, which earned him the reputation of wearing stays. Dressed with fastidious care, he gave the impression of being what he was not – a man of means. He wore a monocle, considered himself interesting, and allowed nothing to interfere with his enjoyment of life. He lived with a mistress, but, as he never took her about with him, he was universally applauded for his discretion.

He declined her offer to sit down, rather as if he were afraid of soiling his clothes, and said in a voice which had a peremptory note in it, because he was here on business and not to waste his time, 'You will forgive me if I come to the point at once, but . . .' He raised his left eyebrow, so that his monocle fell from the ridge of flesh on which it had rested and was caught by him between the fingers and thumb of his left hand. He then glanced at his flat, oblong wrist watch (the cherished memento of a late grand duke) to show that he was extremely busy, and continued:

'We received the address you obtained and our legal adviser, who has consented to act on your behalf, decided that he would pay a personal visit to your husband. Of course he did it as a favour. He is a friend of mine.' He paused to give her an opportunity of acknowledging his favour, but she said nothing. He once more screwed his monocle into his eye.

'Of course, he did not find the gentleman disposed to listen to him, but he did his best to clear up the position. Mr Wilson denies that he married you, although he admitted that he recognised the photograph you gave us. That means that the validity of the marriage will have to be investigated, and it will be impossible to make this a simple case of divorce!' He paused again. Feeling a little uncertain, he wanted to guess from her face what her thoughts were. It was, however, set in an expression of rigid calm, and only the hard lines about her mouth betrayed the effort she made to control herself. A feeling akin to admiration stirred in him, who had known many women, but never one so silent and restrained. A difficult position to be in, but she certainly carried it off well.

'You understand me?' he said. 'Mr Wilson will be charged with bigamy.'

She made a slight movement with her hands. He had several times counted the ornaments in the glass case, beginning always with the wax flowers on the left and ending with the pug dog at the back, before she said:

'Is it inevitable? Could it not be a case of divorce?'

'No, his consent is necessary for that, and presumably he cannot give it because of his . . . wife. You see, it would be almost impossible to keep her out of the evidence.'

Wasn't all this a little heartless? The uneasy thought crossed his mind that he would shrink from remembering this incident.

'Yes, I see.' She rose, and placed a hand on the back of her chair, as though to steady herself.

'Thank you for coming to see me,' she added. He knew that the interview was over, but he was reluctant to go. Something prompted him to say:

'You are trying to shield him, you know. I don't advise it. We must hit hard to win.'

He restrained the impulse to kiss her hand, feeling that the action would be out of place, and surprised that his sophistication should have deserted him. After all, this was the most commonplace affair in the world, and nothing Apouhtin said about the delicacy of the position could persuade him of it, but, in spite of himself, he felt touched. There was that about this woman which evoked his sympathy. Not that he, Zouboff, ordinarily experienced such jejune emotions, but the circumstances almost demanded a little primitive, unsophisticated feeling. Besides, she had a good figure and carried herself well. He admired good carriage in women, and this one walked like an angel. A perfect neck. To kiss it, just where the down began, and there was that little blue vein – ah! So moved that his monocle fell out of his eye, he opened the door for her. There was a slight rustle; he caught sight of a man's figure disappearing down the passage. Someone listening, of course! What infernal holes these boarding-houses were! And what a smell!

He returned to the Society's offices, reflecting on the joys of Maria Ivanovna's lover. These meditations calmed him, and he had so far regained his habitual composure when he reached his study that he exchanged several jokes with his secretary on the folly of mankind in general and of that individual Charles Wilson in particular. 'Well, Vassili,' he said, at last settling down to dictate. 'You had better file this business, but don't get anything mixed up with the American emigration papers, as you did last week. This office work isn't at all your line, or mine for that matter,' he added with a sigh and a smile, as he thought again of that perfect neck, with the little blue vein so clear under the transparent skin.

Meanwhile Mr Panzadski triumphed – Mr Panzadski who moved so softly that one could not hear him, and who had such a winning smile that no one thought twice if they saw him doing anything unusual. If – and he had always been careful that there should be no 'ifs'. That is why he was so very privileged and his triumph so complete. He had slipped away before they had had time to see him, and he possessed such valuable information that, had they seen him, it wouldn't have mattered. He knew his enemy's secret. He could do what he liked with it. For the first time in his life he blessed the fate which had compelled him to learn Russian in the day school at Cracow (forced on him by those brutes!). It had served him in better stead than he could have thought possible. 'I have got you now, my beautiful, my scornful one,' he muttered to himself. When the front door had banged behind Zouboff, and there was no sound in the hall, he extricated himself from the curtain, which hung before a deep recess in the wall, and walked into the sombre dining-room. It was not empty. Mr Jones had retreated there in hasty flight from the derisive, monocled stare which had pierced the rampart of the *Daily Mail*. Mr Panzadski wanted to be alone. He swore under his breath and walked up to the window. But as he looked long and moodily into the garden, where a solitary nursemaid was pushing a perambulator, a thought came to him. His mind was particularly rich in ideas this afternoon! He turned his back on the lace curtain and said:

'Jones.'

Thus startled, Jones dropped his paper.

'I have some interesting news for you. But do not let us be overheard.' With a soft, sidling movement, and a smile on his lips, Mr Panzadski came up to him and began to whisper in his ear. He whispered until Mr Jones's eyes ogled and his jaw dropped. Then, poking his finger with its long, polished nail into the chest where he had set working many emotions, he said, 'Amusing, isn't it?' and quietly left the room.

Thus did he shift the burden of discovery from his own shoulders, and yet again ensured his position as the privileged man, the one foreigner who could be trusted, the peaceful mirthmaker of the boarding-house.

Mr Jones was flabbergasted, but he was also pleased. What luck that he had been in the dining-room when that fellow Panzadski came in! What luck that it was he who had been selected as his mouthpiece! For the whispering had ended with the words, 'You can tell the others, if you like. I shall do nothing about it.' Mr Jones had almost thanked Mr Panzadski for his generosity. For a long time he had hankered for an opportunity to show the others that he was not the fool he looked. Mrs Jacobe had ceased to snub him since she had realised that he knew a thing or two more than she did about that Mrs Wilson. She would respect him now. At last he held the weapon which would make him an important figure in the boarding-house. Another had taken the risks and he was to reap the benefit of them. He had missed parts of the whispering, of course, but he knew enough to rouse their curiosity. 'Bigamy!' He turned the word over and over in his mind. Not divorce, but bigamy. Wasn't it enough to make their hair stand on end?

That evening he could hardly eat his dinner, although in ordinary circumstances it would have been particularly to his taste, and when they were all assembled in the drawing-room he kept putting of the moment when he should reveal his secret. A mixed feeling of vanity and cowardice held him back. Supposing it would fall flat? Supposing they all knew already? The after-dinner topics – Mrs Horner's sciatica, Mr Jacobe's cold, the new income tax rates, that awful murder case at Westbourne – had all been exhausted when the typist's friend gave him the clue.

'I wonder what is the matter with that poor Mrs Wilson,' she said; 'she does look so ill!'

'Matter, I'll tell you what's the matter with her!' The words burst from him so loud that Mrs Jacobe, who had been dozing, positively started into an erect position. That impossible young man again! Really, there was no peace with them.

'She's here to bring a charge of bigamy against her husband. Her lawyer or somebody came to see her this afternoon about it.' He rapped the words out and drew in his breath. He expected something unusual and sudden to happen, but instead of seeing anger and surprise on their faces, he saw only incredulity. There was a silence, during which he was painfully conscious of his clammy hands; then, 'How do you know?' said the commercial traveller.

'Yes, exactly,' echoed Mrs Jacobe, annoyed that it was not she who had made that strictly necessary remark. Mr Jones coloured to the tips of his large, very flat ears. He had not been prepared for this. They had never before doubted his statements. If he told them about Panzadski they would go to him for information; if he . . . Mrs Jacobe's stare disconcerted him. He sought refuge in a lie. 'I heard them,' he said, 'at least I . . .'

But Mrs Jacobe was too quick for him.

'Really, Mr Jones, I am surprised,' she said, speaking very fast, as though afraid that someone would take the words out of her mouth; 'I always believed that one could not hear in the dining-room what was said in here.'

'Cat,' thought Mr Jones vehemently; 'she would have done the same,' but he did not excuse himself. He felt crushed. During all these weeks his own importance had been growing, only to shrink in five minutes like a pricked balloon. Why couldn't he have managed better? If only he had not come out with it like that, but kept them all, especially that shrew, Mrs Jacobe, on tenterhooks. They had hardly listened to him! It wasn't fair! Raging against himself and the whole world, he went out of the room as soon as he decently could. At the door he came upon Mrs James's cat sidling in to get nearer the warmth of the fire. With his neat whiskers and bright, unblinking eyes, it reminded him of Panzadski and he kicked it savagely out of his way.

When he had gone, Mr Richards boisterously slapped his thigh and exclaimed:

'Fine, Mrs J.!' This gross familiarity in so addressing her was a source of continuous vexation, but he was irrepressible. 'You put it well across him, the young cub!'

Mrs Jacobe's head moved twice in acknowledgement of his praise.

'My wife and I both feel that eavesdropping should be strongly discouraged in this house,' said Mr Jacobe's voice from under the palm. 'All the same, you should not have snubbed him quite so hard.'

The actor's wife was speaking. 'He might have told us a lot more.'

'More? What more do you want?' replied Mrs Jacobe in a voice which hinted at the shadowy husband abroad on an interminable tour. 'Isn't this enough? Really, Mrs Freeman!'

Disgraceful to express such curiosity. One couldn't tell how far the woman would go! There was only one way of punishing such laxity.

'Mr Jacobe, let us go upstairs,' she said, and swept from the room, followed by her husband. The others soon dispersed, cowed by the realisation that Mrs Jacobe had been properly roused. Only the cat was left to gaze with unblinking eyes into the flames of the fire.

The uneasiness lasted into the next day. Each member of the boarding-house came down to breakfast with the sense of mysterious happenings about, and on their way to the Underground station the typist remarked several times to her friend that there was something in the air, and what could Mrs Jacobe have up her sleeve? To which the friend rejoined that they would turn that poor Mrs Wilson out of the house, as sure as cats were cats! The restlessness increased during the morning. Whispered conferences were carried on behind closed doors, and the doctor's voice echoed in loud remonstrance over the whole house.

But the cause of this ill-concealed disturbance was unaware of it, so that when Mrs James in a flustered and mysterious way asked if she could speak to her, Maria Ivanovna was completely taken aback. She suspected nothing, because she was too absorbed in her own thoughts to notice how the soft-footed Mr Panzadski had slipped behind the curtain when she came out of the drawing-room with Zouboff. As is often the case with those who live in fear of one thing, she felt no premonition now that a hostile fate had played her false. Mrs James, with a secretive and important look, went into her husband's study and carefully shut the door. It was lunch-time, and the inhabitants, summoned by a crashing gong, could be heard making their way downstairs. One after the other they crossed the landing, and she noticed the heavy tread of the men and the tapping heels of the women. Mrs Jacobe passed with an ominous rustle of silk.

'I just wanted to say, Mrs Wilson,' began Mrs James with a nervous look, 'that I shall have to ask you to make other arrangements . . .' To conceal her uneasiness she pushed with one finger at the carefully trained curls, which lay in a row across her forehead.

'But what do you mean?'

At that Mrs James looked even more flustered and. more miserable. 'You can't stay here now that they all know,' she exclaimed with a note of desperation in her voice. 'I would-n't mind myself, but it's Mrs Jacobe.'

'Yes, I understand now.' It did not occur to her to ask how they knew. It mattered so little. Besides, Mrs James was still talking.

'She's here permanently, you see, and I couldn't very well refuse her. And the others wouldn't like it. It's very awkward,' she concluded lamely. The last person had now passed the door. It was the doctor, making the boards creak under his weight.

'Do you want me to leave immediately?'

'Oh, well, you could finish your week here, while you find yourself somewhere else to go.'

Mrs James was a weak-willed woman, and she was sorry for her lodger, who, as far as she could see, was quiet enough to please anyone, the poor girl! She had even cried this morning when her husband, taciturn after a recent attack of insobriety, had threatened that if she didn't turn the — (he used a word which made Mrs James blush) out of the house, he would do it himself. That was why her eyes were red and puffy, and she was afraid of going down to lunch because that viper Mrs Jacobe, whom secretly she hated more than she feared, would be sure to see that there was something wrong. 'It isn't a bad time of year,' she said, loth to leave the seclusion of the study. 'You"ll find there's plenty of room in the boarding-houses round about here, I should think. It's when the sales come on after Christmas that they all get full up.'

'Yes,' replied Maria Ivanovna. She wanted to escape from the tearful eyes of this fidgeting woman, who continued to stand with her back to the door in an irresolute, hesitating fashion. But before she could say anything Mrs James plucked up courage and, turning round with a loud sniff, said:

'You poor thing! All the same, you are better than all these people downstairs.' She then ducked her head, as if she expected the invisible powers, which had witnessed her lapse, to fell her with one blow, and fled from the room, leaving Maria Ivanovna amazed, alone with the large yellow desk.

Better? she thought. Better than the people downstairs, better than the Jacobes and the impulsive Mrs Freeman and the shy Mr Jones? Perhaps, but to what purpose? To submit to humiliation from the righteous, and receive the callous sympathy of men like Zouboff and Apouhtin. Evil had been forced on her. She had done nothing to deserve its shame, and yet who would clear her from the stigma of another's wrongdoing? She could not escape. She had wanted to at first. When slowly and painfully she had dragged herself out of despair, she had clung to that vain shadow of a hope. She had struggled against the longing, which said, 'Leave it, hide from them, die.' She had forced it back, ignoring the fear which had haunted her even then that to hide and acknowledge herself beaten was the one thing possible for such as her. She was certain of it now. Hadn't all these people, Vera, Apouhtin, Mrs Jacobe, driven her back into that numb, heart-breaking desire, as into a pit from which she had had no right to climb out?

This was her reward for courage! Someone, a long time ago it seemed now, had called her a brave woman. What meaningless words! Why should she be brave if it made her suffer, if by carrying revolt in her soul she could not escape from the nightmare of pain, which bound her with its heavy chain?

As though to banish these thoughts, she put out her hands before her and her palms touched cold wood. She realised that she was leaning against the desk. She was still in the study. She went upstairs and began to pack her things. She walked about the room, concentrating her mind wholly upon each movement she made, because a thought had suddenly flashed on her – a thought so daring and yet so simple that it left her almost breathless, and she could stifle her emotion only by the rhythmical action of folding garments and placing them into her trunk.

III

IT WAS A COLD December afternoon; the sky was heavy with clouds and a slow fog was rising from the river.

Mrs Lucy Wilson came out of the block of flats in which she lived with a tardy wish that she had not chosen this, of all afternoons, to go to Golders Green to see her mother. One could never tell in this foggy weather. She might not be able to get home that night, and her husband wouldn't put the children to bed till goodness knows what hour!

She shivered a little coming out into the heavy cold air of the street. Besides, the thought of her husband made her uncomfortable just now. He had been so strange lately; there was something about the look of him that made her feel unsafe. It would be quite a relief to be with her mother. But perhaps he was only sickening from flu. He was always so careless, going out in the rain without a coat, and one thing and another. . . .

A woman was standing on the pavement outside the house, dressed in black, foreign-looking. She seemed to be waiting for somebody, and she carried a large, rather battered handbag.

Fancy, now! Whom could she know in Michael Mansions? Unless it was that lady on the fourth floor, the lady who'd been to India. Yes, that must be it. She had seen funny people come out of that flat before.

She gave her another look, and walked away with the mincing step she adopted when she thought that her back view was being watched. At the corner she turned round to see the dark figure pass up the steps and disappear in the doorway of the house.

'Tired of waiting,' she thought, as she boarded a bus and was carried away towards Oxford Street.

The stranger walked resolutely into the entrance hall and stopped in front of a board with the names of all the inhabitants on it. She scanned it carefully, and then, as there was a notice on the lift saying 'out of order', she began to mount the stairs. She did it very slowly, pressing the handbag against her body as though to still the beating of her heart. The house seemed deserted. Not a sound came from behind the closed doors she passed. Her steps echoed on the uncarpeted stairs. At last she stopped in front of a door to which a visiting card had been pinned. It was a little soiled at the edges. She read: 'Charles R. Wilson,' and in the left-hand corner '3, Michael Mansions, Bayswater.'

She rang the bell. It twanged somewhere quite near. A moment later she heard approaching footsteps, and a maid in a crumpled apron opened the door.

'Is Mr Wilson in?'

'Oh, yes, Mum, but Missis . . .' She seemed astonished.

'I should like to see him.'

'Will you come in, Mum?'

She followed the girl into a small room, probably used as a study. There was a desk by the window, two leather armchairs, and a dusty bookcase against the wall. Over the mantelpiece hung an engraving, entitled 'Napoleon Bonaparte franchissant les Alpes', in which Napoleon's face wore an expression of abject misery and fear. She noticed it because the light fell straight on this picture, which alone adorned the bare walls. The clock on the mantelpiece ticked with an irregular wheezing sound, as though it were hurrying to catch up lost time. The whole room had a neglected look. Obviously no fire had been lit in the small black grate since last winter. It was very cold.

Charles had profited by his wife's absence to go to sleep on the drawing-room sofa. She never allowed him to do that because she said it looked untidy. Also, she assured him that his snoring (as if he ever snored!) disturbed her. He had just dropped off into uneasy slumber when the maid shouted into his ear that there was a lady to see him. Rating her for not having said that he was out, he laced his boots, and, yawning a little, went into the study.

He opened the door, pushing aside the curtain which was hung there to prevent draughts, and saw a woman standing by the window. There was something familiar about that erect, broad-shouldered figure, something that reminded him . . . His mind, only half-awake, worked feverishly to establish the likeness. Surely this was part of the uneasy dreams which haunted him, part of the fears which assailed him and gave him no rest. So motionless by the window, could it be alive? It was a ghost, a vision of the past which relentlessly preyed upon him. No more than that. He wanted to shut the door and go away, leaving it there to stand and gaze – if it had eyes to gaze with – into the court-yard below. Once he was outside the room it would cease to matter. But then a board in the floor creaked, and as though brought to life by the sound, she turned and faced him. Had he been capable of movement, he would have stepped towards her to take her in his arms, but his feet seemed rooted to the ground. Then something snapped in his bewil-dered brain and he felt horrified that she should be there. Fear and resentment swept over him, and he said:

'What have you come for?'

It was not fair. What business had she to seek him out in his own home after that lawyer had been the other day? Supposing Lucy hadn't gone out? What was he to do, any-way?

And she did not answer him. She only stood with her back to the light so that he could not see her face. This silence was awful. He must say something. They couldn't go on staring at each other like that. Then he heard her voice, low but very clear.

'What have you done?' and again, as if she were echoing someone else's words, 'What have you done?'

He moved closer to the mantelpiece, trying to avoid the look in her eyes: reproachful, pitying, almost tender. If only she would take her eyes off his face. His turn to speak now.

'You forced me into it,' he said, 'you and those damned Russians.'

Useless words, unfair, but it was too late for anything except self-defence. How explain to her what he only dimly understood himself? How tell her that he had meant everything to come right, but that he had slipped back into old ways, daily putting off breaking with his wife, watched happiness slip through his fingers, and shut his mind to the memory of his love for her? Fool that he was: he had not dared face the lesser danger, and now this was on him!

As he stood there, his eyes averted from hers, through the cowardice, which he had not the strength to overcome even now, filtered remorse for what he had done, regret for what he had missed. He thought of her as she had been in Malta – beautiful with a rare intangible beauty which had been like a secret source of life within her. Had he killed it? Furtively his look slid round to her face. It struck him how plain she was, with burning eyes sunk deep into their cavities, and that unhealthy, yellow pallor which somehow accentuated the irregularity of her features. She had changed. He could see no trace of what he had loved in her – the aloofness, the gentle, placid gravity, which had set her apart from others. That wistfulness he had so often compared to the pale light of certain precious stones had vanished. She seemed to him unapproachable, invulnerable, an accusing, relentless spirit, like Nemesis herself.

He realised that the tenderness he had for one moment felt was for a woman he had lost; that for her who stood before him he had only fear and aversion.

'I have come to warn you,' she said, and he fancied that the flame burned more fiercely in her dark eyes. 'You saw that lawyer. You know what it will be, unless . . .' Her voice faltered. It was not till later that he attached importance to that hesitation; then, he only felt stung by her words. Had she come to taunt him with his infamy and her power over him? Was this her revenge for what he had done. She had meant to trap him like this. She had not wanted to spare him one jot of the humiliation she had prepared for him. He turned on her with bitter resentment.

'Is that what you have come for? – to flaunt your virtue in my face, as you have always done? Don't you know that it is you with your goodness who have driven me into this hell? It is your fault that I was afraid of you and couldn't tell you, dared not kill your love. The fear that you would spurn me and treat me like the coward I am, tortured me till I could bear it no longer. It is you, and no one else, who have brought this to pass. Blame yourself. You should have found me out sooner.' He was glad to see her wince; glad that he made her suffer.

'I loved you,' she replied, and, lowering her voice, added in Russian, 'I love you now.'

He started. Was it possible that she meant it?

She went on speaking hurriedly, as though afraid of her own words.

'I cannot bear it. You must not leave me. I cannot tear myself from you. There is still time to repair the wrong you have done. Give me back what you have taken from me: my happiness, my life. They are in your hands; you have left me destitute of everything.'

There was desperate anguish in her voice. Up till then she had seemed lifeless, moving and talking as though in her sleep; but now every nerve in her body was taut with the effort she was making. Her hands gripped the bag she held with such force that her knuckles shone white. She had raised her haggard face, and the merciless light fell on it.

She looked piteous; the fire had died out of her eyes; her lips were compressed in a hard line.

He did not move. Her words stirred no emotion in his heart. She had come too late. He had watched the failure of his life's only attempt at happiness with the despair of a man drowning in a duck pond. After all these months, which seemed to him like long years, of discouragement and self-torture, he could not be loyal to her any more than he had been loyal to Lucy. Better to face the collapse of the lies he had built round these two women and himself and then disappear where nothing would be demanded of him: no love, no duty, no hatred, nothing except utter passivity. He could no longer love her with this suffering between them. His own folly had set them so far apart that now when he saw her again, standing there, divided from him only by a strip of faded green carpet, all he could wish was that she should go away and leave him.

'It's no good,' he muttered; 'I cannot love you.' And with a last effort to excuse himself, added: 'I am sorry, but you shouldn't have come like this.'

The clock on the mantelpiece ticked with an irregular whirr. Maria Ivanovna stood with her eyes fixed on it. It was five minutes to the hour. A few minutes more and the long, tedious silence would be broken by its striking.

When at last it did strike, Maria Ivanovna drew in her breath with a gasp, as though it gave her pain, and went out of the room.

She swept past him so close that the familiar smell of her clothes, the faint perfume of flowers that he knew about her hair, rose to his memory. He stood, unable to take his eyes off the curtain which had fallen back upon her. She had gone – as quietly as she had come. It was right to be quiet and make no fuss.

Suddenly he felt horror at what he had done. He rushed out of the room, wanting to call her back. She must not go; he had not meant to let her go like this. The front door was closed and with nervous, clumsy fingers he fumbled at the latch which, as if on purpose, resisted him. When at last it slid back he ran out on to the empty landing. He dashed down the stairs. Perhaps she had not got to the bottom. There were many flights of them, and she had looked tired, this woman whom he had driven away. In the hall there was no one either. But she could not have gone far. It was foggy outside. He ran this way and that, muttering to himself and peering into the faces of those he met.

Then a woman passed him, hurrying, with head bent down. It must be she – he knew that walk. He seized her hand and drew her towards him.

'Come back,' he said quite loud, so that she should not fail to hear him above the rumble of traffic and the moan of foghorns.

'Come back. I love you, my dear . . . oh, my dear!'

The startled face of an unknown woman stared into his own. He looked at her in speechless horror: then turned away and plunged again into the deceiving yellow darkness.

IV

THE FOG THICKENED. Slowly it sucked air and light into its opaque gloom and hid everything except the round lights of the street lamps, which dimly shone like rows of artificial moons in a night artificially yellow. Shapeless masses twined in and out of the darkness. The roar of traffic sounded like the booming of a distant sea. No familiar sound of wheels or human steps could penetrate through that dull noise. Through that fog people struggled to find their way, sidling like cats along walls and railings, measuring their progress by the lamp-posts, which alone seemed stationary and real in the turmoil of moving shadows.

Through that fog Mrs Lucy Wilson returned home to find her front door open, her husband out, and her children squabbling on the kitchen floor.

Through that fog the second Mrs Wilson wandered aimlessly, not caring where she went, but peering, as if for guidance, into lighted shop windows. She went into one, and the assistant who lounged there, reluctant to go out, served her with alacrity, surprised that there should be anyone left who wanted to buy things. He tried to chat about the weather, for there was a good deal to say on the subject, but she was unresponsive, and only asked her way to the nearest Tube station. Fortunately it was close by.

Crossing the road she was nearly run over by a taxicab, and was only saved from falling under its wheels by a man who pushed her out of the way, and then led her to the other side, with a warning that she must be more careful if she wanted to remain alive.

The trains were crowded and people fought to get in with dogged tenacity, as though afraid that the fog would reach them even here in the airless passages underground. She waited a long time on the platform, till at last she was jostled into a train by the crowd. It was suffocatingly hot in the carriages. Wisps of fog penetrated through the windows and made the air a yellow haze. There was no room to move. Next to her a man, with a bag of tools on the floor between his feet, held his pipe so close to her face that she could feel the heat of it on her cheek. But she did not realise what it was. She was unconscious of every sensation except that of the pain in her head. Although she made attempts to explain to herself what she was doing and why, no clear thought could struggle through her mind. It was as if a thick black curtain had been hung before her. She was cut off from life, and moved through a chimera-like existence in which dark figures flowed in an endless stream all round her. Sometimes she passed them; sometimes they passed her, walking, groping in the uncertain light which swayed above their heads. The train stopped, and because someone at her elbow said, 'Come on; it's Earl's Court,' she pushed her way out and followed more puppet-like figures down corridors and up stairways until she came out with them into Bardolf Road.

The familiar street, which she recognised at once, curving through the fog like a luminous snake, switched her mind back to reality. She knew now that she was outside the entrance to the Underground station, and that in front of her were the hoardings she had passed every day for many weeks. She could see the advertisements as clearly as if there had been no barrier of fog between her and them. On the left, just as usual, there was the Highlander with the plaid over his shoulder; below him a landscape with some cows and a milk-can; further along, a man in shorts riding his tun on the waves; almost out of sight, the chinny youth of 'Climax Collars'; and round the corner, 'Pears' Soap' and 'O'Cedar Mops', with the houses of Metro-land, flanked by the splashy reds and blues of the Olympia Circus.

It seemed to her that rows of these gigantic flat faces were smiling at her with secret irony, like enthroned gods, confident of their powers. They were reproving, mocking her. She could hear them shouting.

'If you had drunk this,' came from the Highlander's grinning lips, 'you wouldn't be wandering here now.'

'Fool, why didn't you use Pears' Soap?'

'Go and live in Metro-land.'

'You would be round and fat if you had eaten Bird's Custard.'

'Read the *Daily Mail*.'

Huge coloured words flashed through her mind. They jostled one another, forming themselves into fantastic patterns . . . Nestle's Milk . . . H.P. Sauce . . . Bass in a red, white and blue triangle . . . Black and White Whisky . . .

They grew larger and larger. She could not drive them away. Was she going mad? What were those dreadful faces and huge hands, pointing at her in derision? She turned and fled, pursued by a havoc of flashing, leaping colours run riot in her brain.

She found the door of the house, because the brass plate on the pillar by the steps shone faintly through the fog. There was no light in the hall. From the drawing-room came the voice of Mr Richards, the commercial traveller, repeating the words which were most often on his lips: 'This rotten Government . . . Why, it's a crying shame . . .' The old, familiar smell of cabbage, dirt and floor polish followed her up the stairs. Only in her room was she free from smells and voices.

No breath of outside life reached her up there. She shut her door, putting a chair against it because there was no lock. Then she took off her hat and coat, and sat down by the table on which she had placed her bag, with a small, heavy parcel inside it. The room was as bare now as when she first came, for she had put away all her things into her old trunk, preparing to leave the boarding-house – 'at the end of the week,' Mrs James had said.

Only that little wooden crucifix still hung on the rail of the bed and the old almanac remained stuck in the frame of the mirror.

She sat watching the fog creep up the window-panes, ooze through the chinks in the wood, hang like fine, yellow smoke along the ceiling. She could hardly see the door now, although the room was so small. Her mind had slipped back into the blind darkness, in which the sharp, throbbing pain in her head was like the pointed, unsteady flame of a gas jet. There was one in her room and it used to flicker with a hissing noise which irritated her. She did not need it now.

The yellow fog gave her light enough.

Somewhere downstairs a clock struck with a thin, wiry sound. Oblivion fled before that faint, plaintive noise, and her mind woke from the inertia which had paralysed it. She remembered how a clock had struck in that room where she had been this afternoon. A clock was striking now. It must be late. Suddenly her head ceased to ache and she began to think rapidly and clearly. Lately she had not been able to think because of that pain, but now it had vanished as if it had been blown out like a candle in a draught. It seemed to her that she had been moving in a chaotic dream for she did not know how long. It might have been hours; it might have been all her life. But now that she understood everything and was no longer afraid, it did not matter. All that she had thought fearful and difficult was so simple and easy. She had been tricked into believing that life was hard; and that the people she had known were evil and wanted to hurt her. But now she knew that they didn't. It was all a mistake she had made because of that awful pain which had tortured her. She smiled as she remembered how Apouhtin, looking at her through his shining spectacles, had said only this morning:

'My dear Maria Ivanovna, you must have courage. You must be brave, as every Russian should be.'

'Brave' – yes, she would be that. She had been foolish and weak, and she had lost herself in a maze of fears; but it was all over now. She was free at last, as Abramovitch had promised. It was that clock striking downstairs that had set her free, waking her from her troubled dream about a dead, barren past.

A strange feeling of contentment stole over her. The weary struggle against something she could not master was at an end. Nothing was left to oppress her; nothing remained alive, except a memory dwelling among loved, forgotten things, which she saw like the delicate, bright-coloured pictures in a kaleidoscope.

She sat reaching out with her mind to all that was dear to her, to all that was outside the fog and the noisy streets, as though she were trying to draw together the filaments which make up the gossamer work of beauty.

Outside, the fog thickened. It defied the walls and the window and darkened the room, bringing with it a smell of damp and smoke. She could hardly see the glass of water on the table and the brown paper of the parcel which her fingers were slowly unwrapping. When it was undone and she felt the smooth leather case, she suddenly lost hold of all the peaceful loveliness which had filled her mind; and dark dreadful memories assailed her so that she almost reeled, clutching the table with her hands. She heard a woman's high, piercing laugh; and through that laugh a voice singing plaintively :

'Ave Maria . . . A . . . ve . . .'

She must forget that voice – it wasn't what she wanted to remember. . . . A clock had struck a short while ago, six . . . seven . . . eight. . . . She clutched at the last shreds of her fast-receding reason. Freedom . . . quickly . . . before this darkness swallowed her up . . . freedom . . . quickly . . . before she forgot that that was her desire.

She rose from her chair and drank some water out of the glass. Then she let down her hair, and, taking a pair of scissors, she cut it off. She placed the heavy, lifeless strands on the table and opened her blouse, so that it left her neck bare. As her hands fumbled with the buttons, she noticed how white her blouse looked against the yellowness of the fog in the room. White, whiter than her bare throat. She was tired. She had done so much today; she must rest, and besides, it was dark . . . time to rest.

Wearily she raised her hands to push up the hair which was heavy on her neck. Motionless she stood, feeling for tresses which were no longer there.

Downstairs in her sitting-room Mrs James heard a sharp report. Her husband! She always knew he would do something desperate. He had come in early this afternoon and had shut himself up in the study. Terrified, she ran upstairs, but the room was empty. She continued her way up, her long skirts catching in the banisters. One after the other she passed the closed doors of her lodgers. Higher, still higher. Yes, at the very top of the house – Mrs Wilson. Her door was closed, too. She tried to open it, but there was a chair against it and something else. She pushed; the chair scraped along the floor till the door suddenly gave way. There was no light, and at first it seemed to her that this room, too, was empty. Then she looked down on the floor and screamed.

The boarders, sitting in their rooms behind closed doors, heard that shrill scream pierce the house from top to bottom. They heard Mrs James scream like one who has lost her reason – because at her feet lay the body of a woman with dark hair, and hands, tenacious in death, clutching her bare throat.

calm, and we discussed certain details. Quite unimportant, really. She was being turned out of her boarding-house because the other boarders objected.'

'English charity! What have I always told you?' interrupted the Princess, who never let slip an opportunity of convincing others of what she firmly believed – that the English were cold-blooded, cruel hypocrites. Engrossed in his own story, he ignored her remark.

'She left me in a very resigned frame of mind. I convinced her that everything was going on quite well and that the only thing needed was patience. I did my best to calm her. And when she had gone (Kadouchkin, our new porter, you know, wanted to show someone else up, but I said, "No, I must have a few minutes' rest; let them wait") I discovered that the springs of the chair on which she had sat were broken. The whole seat had given way. You know what a bad omen that is. In the evening she was dead.'

Murmurs of astonishment circulated round the room. The Princess raised her eyes to the ceiling, as if there she would find an explanation.

'The hand of God,' she said, and Apouhtin nodded. 'Yes, she was a heavy, well-built woman, but the chair could not have broken under her. It's that large, leather armchair in my study. Zouboff, you saw it?'

Zouboff, so immaculately dressed that everything about him, from his collar to the pointed toes of his boots, shone with a subdued, distinguished light, frowned with that part of his face which was not engaged in supporting his monocle, and acquiesced. He had himself examined the chair. It was certainly remarkable.

'What a misfortune,' cooed the Princess in a plaintive voice. 'I do sympathise with you, Feodor Sergeivitch. It must be terrible for you.'

'It's disgraceful that such things should be allowed to happen,' whispered the Prince, whose voice in the winter never rose above a hoarse mutter. He had a permanently bad cold. 'These hysterical women behave goodness knows how, and then expect people like you, Feodor Sergeivitch, who are busy and concerned with important matters, to get them out of the ridiculous situations in which they place themselves. I refuse to pity them.' He looked round gloomily and folded his mouth into its habitual droop.

'*Prince, je suis de votre avis!*' ejaculated the president's sister, who sat perched on a chair like some grey bird with ruffled feathers. '*L'affaire de ma nièce . . .*'

Apouhtin's eyes moved uneasily behind his thick spectacles. His sister had the most reckless, inconsiderate way of talking about family matters in front of guests. He had reproved her often enough, but she was incorrigible. There was an awkward silence, because everyone remembered very well how difficult the position had been at the time. The Princess had, on the strength of the difficulty, refused an invitation to dinner. Andreev passed a plump white hand across his lips to conceal his smile. Zouboff took his monocle out of his eye and dusted it with his handkerchief.

Madame Grigorieff, who considered herself a woman of tact, was the first to speak.

'And how did she kill herself?'

'Oh, horrible!' The consul adjusted his spectacles. 'She shot herself by putting the pistol into her mouth.'

'Very brave,' came from Grigorieff, who was considered a clever, discriminating man, because he always spoke in monosyllables. 'We talk too much,' was a favourite maxim frequently quoted in proof of his astuteness.

'Perhaps,' conceded Apouhtin, 'but it makes it no easier for us. The whole affair must be kept out of the papers, because publicity is most undesirable. I cannot tell you how strongly I feel about this. Our position . . .'

Zouboff interrupted him.

'Why, the individual who played the husband so successfully will find himself a famous man. . . . The English Bluebeard ! . . . think of it!'

The men laughed. Even the Prince let hoarse sounds escape from his throat.

'An easy way to fame,' emarked Grigorieff. *'Tout à fait Byronien,'* he added, turning to Apouhtin's sister, whom he considered an intelligent woman.

'Gentlemen, this is not a matter to joke about,' said the mournful voice of the Princess. 'I feel the disgrace of this woman very deeply, as I am sure you must, and as I know our dear Feodor Sergeivitch does. Such immorality should be punished by man as well as by God. My mind shrinks from the thought of that miserable wretch. He ought to suffer all his life, but of course' – she rapped with her knuckles on the table – 'they will do nothing about it because she was a Russian. That is how they treat us!'

'In our position one can expect nothing else,' said Apouhtin severely. 'I am a man without prejudice, and with lifelong experience, and I warn you' – he shook a finger in front of his own face – 'that if this affair gets into the papers anything may happen. As it is, last year the Society nearly had to close its offices.'

Madame Apouhtin, thinner than ever in a dress which bared her bony shoulders and flat chest, raised languid eyes to her husband's face, and with a slight gesture of impatience, as though she were chasing a fly off her nose, said:

'Don't let us talk about it any more. It is all terribly sad. Poor girl, how she must have suffered!'

'We all talk . . .' began Grigorieff, but his wife cut him short.

'The person I am sorry for is the landlady at the boarding-house. One really can pity her,' she said, in a tone slightly querulous, because she was beginning to feel hungry and had little sympathy for the erring dead.

'Well,' said Apouhtin, protruding his chest and placing his hand over his watch-chain, 'at least there is the satisfaction of knowing that we did our best. I do not believe I flatter myself in saying that I comforted and upheld her to the last. With all my heart I tried to prevent such a deed of violence, but we cannot work against Providence. We have the testimony of the broken chair.'

And as though to prove that a benign Providence did exist to bestow on them the comfortable things of this world, the white-gloved George appeared in the doorway to announce dinner. Madame Apouhtin rose and led her guests downstairs.

'And of course,' added Apouhtin, lowering his voice and taking Grigorieff's arm, 'the whole affair must remain as secret as possible. The woman is dead, it is true, but we must make every effort to keep it out of the papers.'

ABOUT THE AUTHOR

Her nephew writes:

'H. DU COUDRAY' was the *nom de plume* originally used by Hélène Héroys. For the purposes of this edition we have retained the surname, but revealed her sex by using her real first name.

Hélène Héroys was descended from a French family that had moved to Russia under Catherine the Great in the late eighteenth century. She was born in 1906 in Kiev, then part of the pre-revolutionary Russian Empire, where her father Boris was on a military posting. He was a Guards officer – who, incidentally, while at the elite Corps des Pages had served as personal page to the last Empress of Russia at her wedding in 1894. He became a general during the First World War, and was a close witness of the events that led to the disintegration of the Empire in the Bolshevik Revolution of 1917.

Hélène's earliest education was in St Petersburg, but her father had the foresight to send her with her mother and her younger brother abroad to friends in Finland and then Sweden in 1916, just before the Revolution broke out. Her father remained in Russia after the abdication of the Tsar, and met Kerensky and later Trotsky. After the Bolsheviks made peace with Germany and turned on the 'White' officers he was forced to go underground, eventually escaping on foot with one suitcase into Finland. He rejoined his family and they all came to England, as a result of a posting to London by the counter-revolutionary forces.

Thus Hélène arrived in England at the age of twelve, speaking Russian and French and some Swedish, but no English. When the counter-revolution foundered her family became virtually destitute. She managed, however, to complete her education in England and to go to Lady Margaret Hall, Oxford, in 1925 where she read English. In 1927 she won the (Oxford and Cambridge) University Novel Competition Prize with *Another Country*.

After Oxford she did some translation work in England and France, and wrote two further novels, *The Brief Hour* (1930) and *Electra* (1933), and a biography of Metternich (1935). She settled in Geneva in 1936 where she spent the rest of her life, working as a simultaneous trilingual interpreter at international conferences in Geneva and around the world. A longer novel, *The Witnesses*, describing major events of the Russian Revolution, was published in 1967 under a new *nom de plume*, M. W. Waring. She never married. She died in Zermatt in 1971.

CH, London 2003

In the obituary of Hélène Héroys for the Lady Margaret Hall record, one of her Oxford friends who 'admired and loved her' writes of 'Hell', as she was known to them, that 'owing to her passion for anonymity many of her old friends must have remained ignorant of the final flowering of her early promise'. Many, too, will not have known that in 1947 this exotic, passionate, mysterious woman, an international interpreter who dressed in black and smoked Russian cigarettes from a long holder, had become the personal guardian of a thirteen-year-old Spanish girl, Carmen, as part of an American-sponsored scheme. In echoes of Hélène's own story, Carmen had been forced as a young child to flee over the Pyrenees from Franco's Spain with her Communist father. To the end of her life Hélène cherished this girl, for whose education and training as a nurse she paid. She became godmother to Carmen's daughter, who was named after her. But she never introduced this acquired young family to her own family of origin, from whom she had become estranged.

A final vignette from Easter 1949: 42-year-old Tante Hélène feeds cheese fondue in a smart Geneva restaurant to Carmen and the two teenage daughters of the friend from Oxford. Together they attend a League of Nations debate, where Hélène interprets French/English/Russian. Next morning all four are rolling coloured eggs and themselves down the snowy slopes of a Swiss mountain village. A Happy Easter indeed!

EM (one of the teenagers), London 2003

UNCUT DIAMONDS a selection of new writing
Edited by Maggie Hamand

Vibrant, original stories showcasing the huge diversity of new writing talent in London. They include an incident in a women's prison; a spiritual experience in a motorway service station; the thoughts of an immigrant cleaning houses; a child's eye view of growing up in sixties Britain, and a lyrical West Indian love story. Unusual and sometimes challenging, this collection gives voice to writers whose experiences are critical to an understanding of contemporary life in the UK, yet which often remain hidden from view.

Featuring Nathalie Abi-Ezzi, Pam Ahluwalia, Michael Chilokoa, Steve Cook, Belgin Durmush, Alix Edwards, Nick Edwards, Douglas Gordon, Donna Gray, Fatima Kassam, Denese Keane, Aydin Mehmet Ali, Dreda Say Mitchell, Stef Pixner, Katharina Rist, Anita Tadayon, Monica Taylor, Pamela Vincent, Joy Wilkinson.

£7.99 ISBN 1 904559 03 4

THE THOUSAND-PETALLED DAISY
Norman Thomas

Injured in a riot while travelling in India, seventeen-year-old Michael Flower is given shelter by a doctor in a white house in an island on a river. There, accompanied by his alter ego (his glove-puppet Mickey-Mack), he meets Om Prakash and his family, a tribe of holy monkeys, and Lila, the beautiful daughter of a diplomat. Unknown to him, the house is also the home of a holy woman. When she grants him an audience, Michael unwittingly incurs the jealousy of her devotee, Hari, and violence unfolds. A storm, a death and a funeral, the delights of first love and the beauty of the Indian landscape are woven into a narrative infused with a distinctive, offbeat humour and a delicate but intensely felt spirituality.

Norman Thomas was born in Wales in 1926. His first novel, *Ask at the Unicorn*, was published in 1963 in the UK and the USA to critical acclaim. He lives in Auroville, South India.

£7.99 ISBN 1 904559 05 0

ON BECOMING A FAIRY GODMOTHER
Sara Maitland

'These tales insistently fill the vison'—*Times Literary Supplement*
'Stay curious. Read Maitland. Take off'—*Spectator*
£7.99
ISBN 1 904559 00 X

Fifteen new 'fairy stories' breathe new life into old legends and bring the magic of myth back into modern women's lives. What became of Helen of Troy, of Guinevere and Maid Marion? And what happens to today's mature woman when her children have fled the nest? Here is an encounter with a mermaid, an erotic adventure with a mysterious stranger, the story of a woman who learns to fly and another who transforms herself into a fairy godmother.

IN DENIAL Anne Redmon

'This is intelligent writing worthy of a large audience'—*The Times*
'Intricate, thoughtful' —*Times Literary Supplement*
£7.99
ISBN 1 904559 01 8

In a London prison a serial offender, Gerry Hythe, is gloating over the death of his one-time prison visitor Harriet Washington. He thinks he is in prison once again because of her. Anne Redmon weaves evidence from the past and present of Gerry's life into a chilling mystery. A novel of great intelligence and subtlety, *In Denial* explores themes which are usually written about in black and white, but here are dealt with in all their true complexity.

LEAVING IMPRINTS Henrietta Seredy

'Beautifully written . . . an unusual and memorable novel'—Charles Palliser, author of *The Quincunx*
£7.99
ISBN 1 904559 02 6

'At night when I can't sleep I imagine myself on the island.' But Jessica is alone in a flat by a park. She doesn't want to be there – she doesn't have anywhere else to go. As the story moves between present and past, gradually Jessica reveals the truth behind the compelling relationship that has dominated her life. 'With restrained lyricism, *Leaving Imprints* explores a destructive, passionate relationship between two damaged people. Its quiet intensity does indeed leave imprints. I shall not forget this novel'— Sue Gee, author of *The Hours of the Night*